HOW TO TELL
IF YOUR FROG
IS DEAD

~Stories~

Essential Prose Series 162

Canada Council **Conseil des Arts**
for the Arts **du Canada**

ONTARIO ARTS COUNCIL
CONSEIL DES ARTS DE L'ONTARIO

an Ontario government agency
un organisme du gouvernement de l'Ontario

Canadä

Guernica Editions Inc. acknowledges the support of the Canada Council
for the Arts and the Ontario Arts Council. The Ontario Arts Council
is an agency of the Government of Ontario.

We acknowledge the financial support of the Government of Canada.

HOW TO TELL IF YOUR FROG IS DEAD

~ Stories ~

Julie Roorda

GUERNICA
EDITIONS
TORONTO • BUFFALO • LANCASTER (U.K.)
2019

Michael Mirolla, editor
David Moratto, cover and interior design

Guernica Editions Inc.
1569 Heritage Way, Oakville, (ON), Canada L6M 2Z7
2250 Military Road, Tonawanda, N.Y. 14150-6000 U.S.A.
www.guernicaeditions.com

Distributors:
University of Toronto Press Distribution,
5201 Dufferin Street, Toronto (ON), Canada M3H 5T8
Gazelle Book Services, White Cross Mills
High Town, Lancaster LA1 4XS U.K.

First edition.
Printed in Canada.

Legal Deposit—Third Quarter
Library of Congress Catalog Card Number: 2019930491
Library and Archives Canada Cataloguing in Publication
Title: How to tell if your frog is dead : stories / Julie Roorda.
Names: Roorda, Julie, author.
Series: Essential prose series ; 162.
Description: First edition. | Series statement: Essential prose series ; 162
Identifiers: Canadiana (print) 20190048964 |
Canadiana (ebook) 20190048972 | ISBN 9781771833646 (softcover) |
ISBN 9781771833653 (EPUB) | ISBN 9781771833660 (Kindle)
Classification: LCC PS8585.O683 H69 2019 | DDC C813/.6—dc23

*No frogs were harmed in the
writing of this book.*

Contents

HOW TO TELL IF YOUR FROG IS DEAD

~ Stories ~

How to Tell if
Your Frog is Dead

The African clawed frog is native to sub-Saharan Africa where it resides in stagnant pools and backwaters. Provided you construct a vivarium with conditions simulating this natural environment, these frogs can thrive in captivity and make excellent pets. The word *vivarium* is derived from the Latin *vivus,* meaning "to live." Cared for properly, a pet frog may live for up to fifteen years, and your child will enjoy the benefits of interacting with an exotic species while learning valuable lessons about commitment and responsibility. But if you fail to maintain the delicate balance of conditions required for life inside the vivarium, your frog may die.

Although African clawed frogs breathe air, they spend most of their time underwater. The water must be kept between twenty and twenty-four degrees Celsius. If a hurricane or other extreme weather cuts off your source of electrical power and the water temperature drops below twenty degrees, your frog may die, but your child will learn an important lesson about the effects of climate change.

Be sure the top of the vivarium is covered. If it is not properly sealed and your frog hops out, it could starve, or become dried out before you are able to locate and return it to safety. The bottom of the vivarium must be lined with medium-sized pebbles and stones to create nooks and crannies where your frog can hide. If the stones are too small, your frog may accidentally ingest them; if they are too big, your frog could be crushed or pinned, and may die. Your child will learn attention to detail and the value of moderation.

For optimal health, feed your frog a balanced diet that includes live guppies and crickets. If your child is distressed by the fate of these creatures, take the opportunity to discuss the basic dynamics of the food chain. You may wish to explain that the chicken, fish, or hamburgers you had for dinner all similarly died to become food. Your child may choose to become a vegetarian, in which case nuts and legumes are good alternative sources of protein.

Approximately every two weeks, your frog will shed its skin, which it will usually proceed to eat. This is perfectly normal and not a sign of emotional instability. Sometimes the frog will leave the skin behind, providing your child with a fascinating natural artefact to present at Show and Tell.

The vivarium can be lit by either fluorescent or incandescent bulbs; just remember to turn these off at night. Your child may be tempted to use the vivarium as a nightlight, but if the light remains on, your frog's circadian rhythm will be disrupted and it may die. Either way, your child will learn to distinguish imaginary monsters from the real terrors of living and dying.

If you go away on holiday, you will have to ask a friend to feed your frog and monitor conditions inside the vivarium.

The friend should be paid a reasonable, but not exorbitant, fee for performing these tasks. Demonstrate and review all procedures until you are sure your friend has learned how to properly care for the frog. Still, friends can be lazy and forgetful; your frog may die, and your child will learn a valuable lesson about loyalty and trust. If the frog dies, the friend need not be paid.

Do not allow cats to approach within a metre's circumference of the vivarium. Cats do not generally prey on frogs for food, but they may wish to engage in the type of play your frog will not enjoy. Your frog may die. If your frog dies, do not blame the cat. Cats are cruel and haughty by nature. Moreover, they do not respond to punishment. Attempting to punish your cat will only increase its disdain.

You may wish to introduce your frog to a suitable companion. Male frogs, unlike humans, are usually smaller than their female counterparts, and when they are ready to breed, they sing. Frogs may breed up to four times a year. If you allow them to over-breed, your frogs may die. *Amplexus* is the Latin word used to describe the mating position of frogs. It means embrace. Sometimes a female frog will *amplex* another female, or a male another male. This is nothing to be alarmed about. It is perfectly natural, and your child will learn a valuable lesson about tolerance and diversity.

If your frog dies, do not attempt to flush it down the toilet. Your frog is not a goldfish. It has rather the shape of a rubber plug closely approximating the diameter of the pipe connecting your toilet to the municipal sewer system. Should your toilet become plugged, you will have to call a plumber. The plumber will use a snake to dislodge the clog caused by your frog. You may wish to reassure your child that the plumber will not be sending a real snake into the pipes, such as those seen on YouTube swallowing frogs whole. A plumber's snake is a tool so-named metaphorically, because of its long, sinuous shape and flexibility. Even if it were a real snake, it would only prey on live frogs, not dead ones.

It is best to dispose of your frog by burial in a biodegradable container or wrap. A Q-tip box is ideal, as it allows an open-casket option for mourners to pay their respects. You may wish to conduct a modest ceremony commemorating the life of your frog. A few simple songs would be appropriate, particularly if the dead frog is male. Popular choices include "Let's Go to the Hop" and "It's Not Easy Being Green."

You may wish to mark the frog's grave with a small stone. Be sure the stone is not too small to spot, and avoid, when you are cutting the grass, or it might shoot out the back of the lawnmower, at bullet speed, and your child could lose an eye.

It is inadvisable to disguise or gloss over the fact of your frog's death when you discuss it with your child. If you say the frog has gone to live on a farm, your child will eventually learn the truth and may require expensive therapy. Couching the tragedy in spiritual terms is also unwise. Although some deities have been known to employ a plague of frogs as an agent of wrath, religion is generally silent on the subject of their afterlife.

Before you make any firm plans to bury or memorialize your frog, remember that frogs hibernate for several months of each year. In this state, a frog practically ceases to breathe and its pulse becomes undetectable. Do not attempt to wake your frog. Contemplating this condition of deathlike stillness can be beneficial, particularly if your child is prone to hyperactivity. But even the most careful observation may fail to distinguish between life and death. The only way to know for sure whether your frog is dead is to be patient and wait for spring. If you suspect you have erroneously buried your frog alive, you will have learned a valuable lesson.

Predestination

Leonard fought his way to the back of the crowded street-car, but there were no seats available. As he clung to a pole, the glint of light on a shiny screen in the lap of the woman seated below him caught his eye. She was holding a tablet computer that seemed to be all silver and sparkling glass; it must be the new 3D *i*Ball everyone was talking about, Leonard thought. The woman swished through a series of photographs of swans and ducks, and Leonard recognized the pond in High Park, which he visited every weekend. Next was a close-up of a young woman with light brown hair and wide grey eyes sitting in a restaurant, laughing happily at the photographer. The wall behind her was burnt-orange and there was a bottle of olive oil with a floating sprig of rosemary on the table. Leonard couldn't see the face of the woman holding the tablet, but from the colour of her hair and the way the ends rested in a little half-curve on her shoulders, he knew the photo was of her. Her nose was a tiny bit beaky and the chin a little too small, but she was quite pretty, he thought, in a goofy kind of way, like a Holly-wood actress who only gets the comic roles. She was, in fact, exactly the kind of woman he found most attractive, but could never get up the nerve to ask on a date.

Leonard leaned in closer, but when the woman swished to the next photograph, he snapped his head back so quick-ly it smacked against his own hand on the pole. The photo on the tablet was of him. Leonard. He too was in the res-taurant, smiling widely, having a good time. Then an even more shocking photo of him and the woman side-by-side, leaning in together for the shot, his arm around her shoul-ders. This woman he had never seen before.

Leonard's heart hammered and he broke out in a tepid sweat while his mind raced. It must be someone else, he thought, someone who just looked a lot like him. But on the clear, high-definition screen, even without the special goggles that would render the image three-dimensional, the resemblance was uncanny. His hair was the same, so were the glasses, and he was wearing a polo shirt exactly like the one his mother had given him two weeks ago.

Suddenly, the woman slid the tablet into her bag and jumped from her seat. Panicked that she might see him, Leonard pushed farther back into the streetcar, tripping and stepping on an old man's foot. "Sorry," he muttered. Mean-while the woman made her way to the door and got off. Leonard realized too late that it was his own stop as well. Though shaky and disturbed, he managed to get off at the next stop and walk the three blocks back to his apartment, glancing around him all the while as if someone — the woman — could be watching him.

He lived in a bachelor apartment on the top floor of a

low-rise building. When he stepped off the elevator, he could see that the door to the fire escape at the end of the hall was open, and his neighbour Veronica was at her usual perch.

"Hey, Lenny!" she called.

Veronica was a petite, middle-aged woman with an electric blue streak in her otherwise grey hair. He had no idea how she made a living. She never seemed to go anywhere except out onto that fire escape to dispense neighbourly advice and play fetch with her black cat Sabbath. She would toss a stick over the railing, into the yard behind the building, and the cat would tear down the stairs at break-neck speed, often leaping onto the lawn from as high as the second floor to retrieve the stick and climb back up five flights for Veronica to throw it again. Feeling he could use some guidance, Leonard joined her outside.

"You know how they say everyone has a double," he said.

"Ah yes. The evil twin. Unless, of course, *you* are the evil one," Veronica said. "In which case, meeting your doppelganger could have its advantages."

"I haven't actually met him yet," Leonard said. He told her what he had seen.

"Are you adopted?" she asked matter-of-factly.

"I don't think so."

"Maybe you had a twin that your mother gave up for adoption," she said.

Leonard frowned. "That seems unlikely."

"Seems, schmeems. How often do you hear about some genetics study that is based on observations of identical twins separated at birth? It's the premise of the entire nature versus nurture debate. You'd expect the separation of identical twins to be a rare scenario, but obviously it happens more often than we think, since there appears to be this bottomless pool of potential study subjects. It might even be a conspiracy."

Sabbath slipped between Leonard's ankles and dropped the stick at Veronica's feet. She picked it up and sent it twirling through the air like a baton. The cat raced after it.

"There is another possible explanation," she said. "The old switcheroo."

"What do you mean?"

"Another woman, in the hospital at the same time as your mother, gave birth to twins. Your mother took home one of the twins instead of her own baby. I mean, they all look the same at that age."

"But they would have noticed eventually, the parents with the twins who grew up looking nothing alike."

"Yeah, that would have been awkward." Sabbath nudged her again and this time Veronica tossed the stick up in a high arc before it made its downward turn and the cat reached the ground at the same time. "Was she pretty?"

"Who?"

"The woman in the photos. Don't tell me you didn't notice."

Leonard blushed and turned away from Veronica's smirk. "I think I'll go give my mom a call," he said.

"Give her my regards," Veronica said, who'd never met her.

His mother answered in the middle of the first ring. "Hello-o?"

"Mom, am I adopted?"

"Of course not. You've got my cheekbones and the

famous Woodward pigeon toes, just like your father's entire family."

That eliminated Veronica's switcheroo scenario as well as adoption. The only one left was the abandoned brother. "Would you have liked to have twins?" he asked.

"It's funny that you should ask, because when I was pregnant with you, I really thought there might be two of you."

"Why? Were there two heartbeats?"

"No. And there was no ultrasound back then to confirm these things. It wasn't the doctors who put the idea in my mind, it was your Aunt Martha. You know, the psychic?"

As far as Leonard knew, the only accurate prediction Aunt Martha had ever made was of the famous Mississauga train derailment in 1979, but her reputation persisted. No family celebration was complete without Aunt Martha and her crystal ball.

"Martha told me she'd had a vision of me with twins," his mother said. "She insisted there were twins in my future. The truth is, as delighted as I was with you, I was a little disappointed that you weren't two. It runs in families, you know."

"Twins?"

"Clairvoyance. There's a long history of it on my mother's side. My grandfather was famous for it. Did you know he predicted Hurricane Hazel?"

Leonard had trouble sleeping that night. Every time he closed his eyes, he saw his own face grinning back at him. Would he and his double share personality traits, he wondered — even if they weren't genetically related — or would they be opposites? Good twin, evil twin. Leonard was sure he himself was not an evil person, but he didn't think he was exceptionally good either. He helped out at a food bank a couple of times a year, but he also stole Scotch tape from work.

As he tossed and turned in his narrow twin bed, he mulled about his mother's catalogue of family quirks. Why couldn't he have inherited something useful and exciting, like his Uncle Irving's good looks and suave ease. Women were always falling in love with him. Or his grandmother's musical talent. They said she could have been a champion accordion-player if she hadn't given it all up to get married. Instead, all he'd come by was a genetic predisposition to trip over his own feet. If anything determined his future, it wasn't a quality of good or evil, but that maddening awkwardness.

At the first sign of light outside, he gave up sleeping and made himself some toast; as usual, he cut off all the crusts. This was not because he didn't like crusts, but so that he would have something to feed the ducks in the park. Most of them were mallards and wood ducks, but there was one domestic white duck among them, probably an abandoned pet. The white duck had mated with a male mallard in the spring and now had one hybrid duckling. It remained to be seen whether the duckling would be capable of flying like its wild father, or earthbound like its domesticated mom. All week, Leonard collected his crusts in a Ziploc bag.

After breakfast, he tucked the bag inside his jacket and headed for High Park, a ten-minute walk from his apartment. Aside from joggers and dog-walkers, the park was empty and quiet. As he crested the hill overlooking the pond, a wave of quacking rose from below on the brisk spring air.

At the bottom, he took a trail he knew led to a low bank where the ducks liked to gather. The trail twisted and turned before coming out on to the bank; Leonard realized too late that there was someone already there ahead of him, a woman with a bag of crusts. Ducks, including the hybrid family, crowded around her feet. Leonard's first instinct was to flee back the way he came, but the ducks had already begun to swarm in his direction, sensing another hand-out. The woman turned to look at him and a cold shiver climbed up his back and covered his scalp. It was her, the woman with the photos.

Leonard stared, wondering how she would react to seeing what must be to her, a familiar face. But her expression revealed neither surprise nor recognition. "Good morning," she said pleasantly.

Leonard tried to say good morning back, but it came out as more of a cough.

"You brought some bread as well," she said. "Good thing. They're greedy this morning."

If she wasn't surprised to meet the spitting image of a man she obviously knew well, Leonard wondered, was it possible she was expecting this encounter? Had he been lured into some scheme, a diabolical plot orchestrated by this woman and his evil twin? Maybe she'd been following him, he thought. But she was in the park first. Leonard didn't know what to say or do, so he reached into his Ziploc and began tossing bits of toast to the birds.

"I don't know why I love ducks so much," the woman said. "I always have. I remember in kindergarten we had to pick an animal sticker to put above our coat hooks to remember which one was ours. The others all fought over the cool animals: the cheetahs and crocodiles. But I chose the duck." She looked up at Leonard with such a radiantly goofy smile, that he couldn't help but smile back. "My name's Charlotte, by the way."

"I'm Leonard."

She held out her hand and Leonard reached for it, realizing too late that the traces of butter from his toast had made his hand greasy. He felt himself turn red, but Charlotte didn't seem to notice. The hybrid duckling stepped a webbed foot right on top of her shoe and snatched a piece of bread from Charlotte's hand. Her laughter trilled out across the pond and Leonard's heart fluttered. He was confused. How could he be so attracted to the woman who was quite possibly in cahoots with his doppelganger, planning his demise?

An awkward silence developed, punctuated by quacks. Leonard searched desperately for words that might bring some clarity to the situation, or at least make him look a little less of a bumbling fool. He needed some small talk, some popular topic of conversation. "What do you think of the new *i*Ball?" he blurted.

"Ah! Don't get me started!" Charlotte said. "It's sooooo unfair that we have to wait a whole month longer to get them in Canada than in the States. I'm just dying to get my hands on one."

Leonard stared. His hand inside the bag of crusts trembled. "You haven't got it yet?" he half whispered.

"Of course not!" Charlotte said, laughing. "Nobody does. Not this side of the border. But I've reserved one from the first batch when it arrives. I can't wait. I'm so excited about using the 3D camera!" She emptied the last of her crumbs on the ground. "That's me done."

The hybrid duckling waddled furiously after its mother back to the pond.

"Do you think—" Leonard said, sputtering, gulping, then trying again. "I mean, I'd love to know if the *i*Ball is as good as they predict. Maybe we could get a coffee sometime?"

⚜

The restaurant Charlotte chose for their one-month anniversary celebration was exactly as Leonard had foreseen: burnt-orange walls and a bottle of olive oil with rosemary on each table. Leonard knew exactly which shirt to wear and had no trouble deciding on red wine over white. They passed the brand new *i*Ball back and forth, then handed it to the waiter who gushed over the sleek and sparkling tablet before snapping a photo of the happy couple.

They shared tiramisu for dessert, but after three bites, Charlotte pushed the dish at Leonard and leaned back in her chair, exclaiming that she was stuffed. He continued to eat, gazing at her all the while—he could have stared at her all day. She glanced up as a group of people passed their table. Suddenly a startled look crossed her face.

"Is something wrong?" Leonard asked.

Charlotte waited a few moments until the passers-by were out of earshot then leaned in across the table. "Didn't you see that guy?" she said. "He looks *exactly* like you!"

'Til Death

Who says romance is dead? If you believe that, I guarantee you'll change your mind by the end of this Haunted Tour. Of course, the fact that you've come out for this special Valentine's Day edition suggests I'm probably preaching to the choir, as far as love is concerned, but there are always a few sceptics. Take hold of your sweetie's hand now, and cuddle up close; it's not just the February wind-chill that's going to make you shiver on this trip.

Now if you'll gather around me here, I have a question for you: How many of you carry smart phones? As well as affirming your faith in the undying nature of love, this first example may serve as a cautionary tale. Look around. You may not think there is much to see here, just a typical Toronto back alley, some run-of-the-mill graffiti. There are streetlights, which means it's well-lit at night. But those were no use to a young woman who took a short-cut early one November evening, just a few years ago.

As she entered this intersection with the alley that leads

to the street, she was blowing goodnight kisses to her young lover by videophone. She didn't notice the garbage truck that was barrelling down on her. The driver saw her, honked and tried to stop, but the young woman didn't even look up as she stepped directly into the truck's path. Didn't have a chance. Her boyfriend saw a rush of dark sky and buildings flash across his screen as the woman's phone flew through the air upon impact then clattered to a stop on the ground, where it relayed to the horrified lover one last shot of his girlfriend's feet sticking out from the truck under which she was pinned — a bit like the Wicked Witch of the East's ruby-slippered feet sticking out from beneath Dorothy's house — before his screen went black.

Reports started coming in a few years later, always from people taking the same short-cut after dark. Just as they enter this intersection, their phones ring. When they answer, they hear nothing, but sense a presence and feel overwhelming sadness that makes them certain someone is there at the other end. The calls are always from unknown, untraceable numbers. In at least one instance, the person was sure her phone was turned off, yet it still rang with the ghostly call.

I can see several of you nervously patting your pockets, but don't worry, the ghost only calls if you are in this alley alone. Those who have just parted from a lover are particularly vulnerable. So stick together, look both ways, and there'll be no ghost calls tonight. Shall we move along?

This is a charming little church, more than a hundred and fifty years old. There's no need to go inside, but if you'll just stop here in this courtyard, I'd like you to listen very carefully. Do you hear that? A kind of grinding noise—it's faint, but quite distinct—like the sound of a handsaw cutting wood. No? Perhaps the wind is making it difficult to discern. You need a more practised ear, like mine.

Although it now belongs to the Unitarians, this church originally housed a Lutheran congregation. Many of the couples who married here were of German descent, and the Germans had a tradition requiring the newlyweds, upon exiting the church, to saw through a log together to signify the beginning of life-long partnership and cooperation in even the most mundane and practical aspects of life. Couples took part in this meaningful ceremony for centuries, and aside from the odd severed pinkie, it was entirely safe.

Not so for one unlucky couple in the 1920s. The bride created a bit of a sensation by wearing a long lace veil—they weren't a common fashion with regular people back then, especially among austere Lutherans, but this young woman was a trendsetter. The couple were full of joy and energy as they began sawing through the log at record speed, obviously perfect life companions. Then disaster—the lace of her veil caught in the teeth of the blade and yanked her face down against the log where the saw sliced clear across her throat, severing the jugular. It happened so fast, witnesses could hardly fathom what they'd seen, least of all the poor groom whose last lusty heft on the saw had whisked his beloved away from him forever. But the groans of that saw —some say they almost resemble sobs—can still be heard today, forever echoing the memory of young love cut tragically short. Forgive the pun.

If you'll follow me across the street here, I'll tell you what I believe is an even more romantic story. Although it resembles a church, this neo-Gothic building we're entering now is part of the university, hence strictly ecumenical. You can imagine the wide variety of traditions this chapel and banquet hall have seen. About ten years ago, a young couple of Iranian descent held their wedding ceremony here. The Iranians have a touching custom in which the newlyweds lick honey from each other's fingers so that their life together will start sweetly. Unfortunately, in this case, one of the bride's false nails came loose in the groom's mouth and he choked to death in front of her eyes. Tragic, yet beautiful.

Ghost Hunters International has compiled statistics that prove people are seven times more likely to die on their wedding day than on any other. But don't let that discourage you. That's what it's all about, isn't it? Love is worth dying for—I should know, I've buried three wives myself. But you may not want to marry in this particular chapel. Many guests have reported finding mysterious scratches on their bodies after attending a ceremony here.

Zip up your coats, we're going to head back out and down the street a ways. Here we are. Yes, that's right, a children's playground—not the kind of place you want to hear about ghost sightings. I can assure you this particular ghost has never been spotted during the day, only after nightfall, so your children can continue to play here without fear of being spooked.

What I want to show you is the wading pool. It's empty now, of course, for the winter, but I'm going to tell you about one summer evening, shortly after the pool was constructed, about forty years ago now. Toronto was experiencing a heat wave and the pools all stayed open later than usual. But eventually, dusk arrived and a city worker, a man in his fifties, came to drain the dirty water. He'd recently celebrated his twenty-fifth wedding anniversary for which his wife had given him a gold identity bracelet. The truth is, he wasn't that keen on the bracelet, found it a bit fussy and feminine, but he loved his wife dearly and wore it every day with pride.

You can imagine it was to his great dismay that evening when, just as he reached into the last bit of water to clear some grass from the drain, the clasp on the bracelet opened and it followed the water down. Desperate, the man reached down into the pipe as far as his arm would go, lying down on the ground to reach deeper. What he didn't realize was that a valve, just a few inches down would close automatically once the draining was complete. Severed his arm just below the shoulder.

Since then there have been several reports, usually from young lovers liaising in the playground after dark, of a ghostly hand reaching up out of the drain, clenching and unclenching the fingers as if it's trying to grab on to something. Some accounts describe the arm as wearing some kind of shiny bracelet; others say it is completely bare. If you look closely now, you may just be able to see its outline. No? It's a bit difficult with the swirling snow. Learning to perceive the ghosts we share our planet with is a skill that takes practice, but there's no reason why you can't learn.

What's most interesting about this case is that the man in question survived the accident — albeit minus a limb — and lived another twenty years. Yet sightings of the ghost arm began within months of the event. It's as if the arm possessed a ghost of its own. I reported it to Ghost Hunters International and they said such visitations by phantom body parts are not unusual at all. I had my gall bladder removed a few months ago. I'm really looking forward to its manifestation in spirit form once it has grown accustomed to its new circumstances. It may have something very interesting to report, which I will, of course, incorporate in future tours.

I thought it would be appropriate to end at the most romantic of the sites — this charming little house. Though it's abandoned and boarded up, people swear it gives off twinkles of light from time to time, usually in winter. You might catch some glimmers now, if you look closely. It was a young couple's starter home, and they wanted to make their first Christmas here perfect, so on a snowy evening not unlike tonight, they came outside to decorate the front porch with a string of coloured bulbs. They managed to attach the string to the roof, but when the young man went to plug it in at an outside socket just near the ground, something went terribly wrong.

The outlet was severely corroded, as it hadn't been used in years, and when his hand, wet with the snow, came in contact, it sent a jolt of electricity through his body so strong it killed him in seconds. It is unclear whether his wife grabbed hold of his hand because she saw what was happening and preferred dying with him to being left alone, or if they'd just never let go to begin with. The two were found the next day, burnt to charcoal, buried in a layer of fresh snow, their hands fused together for eternity.

Happy Valentine's Day, folks. I hope you'll all return for another of my themed ghost walks. I'm planning an absolutely unforgettable tour for Mother's Day, starting at the laundromat next door, where a young mother playing hide-and-seek with her child concealed herself inside a mega-washer. No one knows exactly how the machine was turned on, if it was a crime or a dreadful accident. But the appliances have been known to start up on their own in the wee hours ever since. I promise the whole tour will be equally scintillating. What better way to celebrate the woman who gave you life?

Wheel

It stopped. Why did it stop?

— Maybe we're stuck.

— We can't get stuck here. We're right at the top!

— Someone has to be.

— Is this part of the initiation?

— It's not an initiation. It's a staff morale booster. It was my idea. I used to come to this fair when I was a child. It always marked the beginning of summer.

— I don't think they've serviced this Ferris wheel since.

— Why did you apply for a job at the CN Tower if you're afraid of heights?

— I'm not really afraid of heights, I just … oh no …

— Don't look down. It's worse if you look down. Look at me instead. You know, your eyes are the most amazing green.

— I'm not working at the top of the tower. Only at the ticket counter.

— You'll be promoted quickly, I'm sure. I was promoted after only a month.

—Did you have to work at the top?

—No, no. I've always worked in the Tour-of-the-Future complex in the basement. I started out as a lowly passport issuer, but soon worked my way up to shuttle pilot.

—Why do you call yourself that? You're not really a space shuttle pilot. It's a flight simulator. You're an actor.

—A good actor lives his role. We want to create a convincing experience of future technology for our passengers. If I don't believe it, how can I expect them to?

—I don't think they actually believe they're on a space shuttle flight to Jupiter. It's just a fun ride. Like this Ferris wheel was supposed … oh no, I think—

—Are you going to be sick? You can hold my hand, if you want.

—It's okay. I'm fine. Just don't swing the seat.

—Think about something completely unrelated to the situation. Think about pancakes. No, wait. Pancakes are bad if you're feeling queasy. Something different. Wow, it's hard to think of something unrelated to the present circumstances. Like trying not to think of an elephant. That's it! An elephant. Or better yet, think of a sloth. That's what I do when I'm about to go on stage and I'm really jumpy and nervous. I imagine the slow, calm life of a sloth.

—I know.

—You know I imagine sloths?

—I knew you were going to say that. I'm having a déjà vu. It started when you said pancakes.

—It's still happening?

—Yes.

—What am I going to say next?

—Something about a waffle iron.

—That's so freaky! I was just thinking about a waffle iron my mother used to have. When I mentioned the pancakes I thought of it. I wonder if she still has it.

—That's it. It's finished. The déjà vu is over. I have no idea what comes next. I wish I did. Then I'd know if we're ever going to get down from here.

—Seriously, that was really weird. You read my mind.

—No, I didn't. I only read my own mind. Or remembered it.

—You remembered knowing the future?

—I don't know. You *thought* about the waffle iron, but would you have mentioned it if I hadn't first?

—You tell me.

—I either remembered having the conversation before, or I remembered having a premonition of the conversation.

—What's the difference?

—One travels back in time, the other travels forward.

—That's deep. Or am I just confused? Wait. Are you saying that it's possible you've travelled here from the future?

—I don't think so. Wouldn't I know if I was visiting from the future? Unless I was visiting just for the duration of the déjà vu, then left again. But why would I choose that particular moment?

—There must be something significant about it.

—About pancakes and waffle irons?

—Maybe the waffle iron thing is symbolic. It was a kind of "waffle moment," a glitch in time. Maybe time actually stopped momentarily— that's why the Ferris wheel stopped turning.

—Then why didn't it start again when my déjà vu ended?

—Good point. Well, maybe it's not the words that are

significant, but the moment. Us two here together ...
the fact that we just met ... you know, fate and all that.

—Oh crap! Did you feel that?

—What?

—I think we moved. Oh, no! I shouldn't have looked down.

—Breathe. Take deep breaths. You can put your head on my
shoulder if you want.

—It's okay. I'm all right now. Just don't swing the seat.

—Look. The lights on the CN Tower just went on. I love that
tower. It's such a great symbol of progress and optimism
about the future.

—Not really. It's older than me. Probably even older than
you.

—Still. It gives me hope. Hope that one day I will finally
realize my dream. Play all the great roles on the stages
of the world. What do you hope for?

—I just hope I get down from here alive.

—Look, there's a crowd forming. Maybe they'll hold out a
blanket for us to jump into.

—Don't even joke about that. Oh no!

—Sorry, I shouldn't have told you to look down.

—No. It's starting again.

—Nausea?

—Another déjà vu. I can't believe this! It started when you
said blanket.

—Really?

—I knew you were going to say that. Now you're going to
say that's freaky.

—That *is* freaky.

—Finished. What do you think it means?

—When I was a child, many moons ago I admit, someone

told me that déjà vus were experiences that we dreamed about sometime in the past, but didn't remember when we woke up. We only remember when we actually experience them.

—But whether you dream it while sleeping or have a premonition while awake, either way, the mind is accessing information from the future. How does that happen? And why?

—You're very smart, aren't you? Smart and beautiful.

—You know, when I was little ... no, it's too silly.

—Please, you can trust me. You're too beautiful to be silly.

—When I was little, I used to wake up in the middle of the night and there was a man in my room.

—Oh no! Someone broke in?

—No, no, nothing like that. I say I woke up, but I probably just dreamt that I was waking up. But it happened all the time. He wore a long tunic or gown and a dome-shaped hat with a brim that bent straight up, like a sailor's cap, and all of it was a luminous, deep-sky blue. It made me think of the word *raiment*. Angels and transfiguration. That's how I started to think of him. As *Raiment*, like that was his name.

—Did he say anything?

—We had these long conversations. I don't remember what any of them were about, just that they seemed very important. I felt important and grown-up, though I could never say why.

—Is that all you did? Talk?

—Sometimes he walked around the room, his hands clasped behind his back. But usually he just sat on my child-sized desk chair — without ever breaking it. And yes, we just talked.

—I'm glad you told me that. Though I don't know what it means.

—When I had déjà vus when I was little, I remember thinking they were connected to something Raiment had told me. But why would he visit like that to discuss trivialities? There must be some significance. Two déjà vus so close together?

—It's probably just stress.

—You don't think it signals something momentous about this night, like, maybe it's my *last* night. Maybe I'm *not* going to get down from here alive!

—I'm sure it doesn't mean that. But if it does, at least we're together. Let me put my arm around you, you're shivering.

—I'm okay. I'm fine. Just don't swing the seat.

—Oh look, a fire truck. I wonder if that ladder's tall enough.

—Oh no!

Beside Herself

"**I** just don't feel like myself," Melissa said.

"Maybe you're experiencing a walk-in," said Charles, her husband.

"As in closet?"

"No. A walk-in refers to the soul who steps into a body and personality to take the place of the original soul that the person was born with. Usually, of course, the departure of a soul requires the person's death, but in exceptional circumstances, a new soul will *walk in*, allowing the person to continue living,"

Melissa thought this unlikely. "Maybe it was the scallops," she muttered.

"It happened to me, you know," Charles said. "A new soul took over me."

"When?" asked Melissa.

"About a year ago. When I was going through that hard period."

"That hard period? You mean when you were having an affair with my sister."

"Melissa, we've been through this. It's over. Thanks in part to this new soul, in fact, I'm working through the issues and challenges inherent in my personality and body, the things I'm supposed to work on in this particular incarnation. I'm healing. You should too. I don't know why you don't take my advice and start meditating. It's worked wonders for me. Given me a whole new perspective."

"You're sure it wasn't the organic contact lens fluid?"

"Would you prefer I continue to bathe my eyes in dangerous chemicals? You shouldn't be so dismissive of everything. Think about it, you got a new husband out of all this."

"Does that mean I cheated too, on my old husband, now that I've got this new strange one? I suppose that makes you feel less guilty, does it?"

"Guilt is a useless emotion," Charles said. "Besides, a walk-in soul is not just some stranger. It usually has an intimate connection to the soul it's replacing. They may have been lovers in a previous life, or parent and child. Possibly even in one's current life."

"So who am I sleeping with?" Melissa asked. "Your father?"

Charles laughed boisterously. "That's impossible! It can only be someone from your current life if that person has already died, and my father is very much alive. Have you forgotten last weekend?"

"He may be alive, but he has no soul," Melissa grumbled. She had spent the entire visit dodging her father-in-law who patted her backside at every opportunity. Like father, like son.

"The old bastard," Charles said, sighing fondly.

"And did this walk-in occur before or after the affair with Chelsea?" Melissa asked.

"It was during. I knew I had to end it, but I didn't quite have the strength or the wherewithal until the new soul stepped in."

"Great! So both of you slept with my sister."

"Melissa, at some point you're going to have to accept the past for what it is: the past. There's no other way to move on. I sometimes wonder if there isn't something else going on here."

"Something other than your cheating?"

"Like maybe you've always been jealous of your sister. She is a beautiful woman."

"We're identical twins — she looks exactly like me!" Melissa shouted.

"I'm not just talking about physical beauty," Charles said. "I refuse to fight with you anymore. I've got a big day tomorrow. Taking the kiddies to the chocolate factory. So I'm going to bed early. Are you coming?"

"No," Melissa said. While Charles headed upstairs, she locked herself in the bathroom. Physically she and Chelsea were nearly indistinguishable from each other, but in every other way they were polar opposites. It was Chelsea who introduced Charles to all this New Age stuff — meditation, past life regressions, tarot cards. After nearly causing the break-up of Charles and Melissa's marriage, and apparently driving Charles' old soul from his body, Chelsea was now, as she described it, *directing Charles' program of healing.* She'd offered to develop a program for Melissa as well, but Melissa stopped speaking to her when she learned of the affair. She wondered if Chelsea got a commission for all the meditation classes and spiritual counsellors she'd recommended to Charles. They were expensive, but Charles shelled out for them all.

Charles didn't have a clue about money; he was bad with numbers of any kind. When he landed a permanent teaching job, he was relieved it was only Grade One, because he could never remember how to do long division. Melissa was the one who filed their income tax returns, dealt with the bank and paid all the bills, and she was the one bringing in the lion's share of the cash. They'd bought their house at the height of the market; Charles' teaching salary wasn't even enough to cover the mortgage. Melissa had set herself up as an independent marketing consultant after being laid-off by an agency a few years ago. At first, things had gone amazingly well and she was making more money than ever. But then the recession hit and clients started to cut back. Unbeknownst to Charles, Melissa had already used all their savings and RRSPs. So while Charles worked on his healing program and fulfilling incarnational goals, Melissa worried.

She stared in the bathroom mirror and seemed to be seeing two overlapping images of herself. She closed her eyes and opened them again. Still seeing double. Am I having a stroke, she wondered. Her stomach gurgled; her insides felt like they were shifting about. She washed her face with a cold cloth.

Charles was sitting in bed reading, with his iPod in his ears, when Melissa passed the bedroom. She opened the door to the attic and crept up. At the top of the stairs was a sign Charles had posted saying "No cell phones beyond this point" that Melissa ignored. Charles had painted the attic ceiling that slanted all the way to the floor midnight blue. It took four coats to get a solid colour, then he'd pasted on hundreds of glow-in-the-dark stars. When Melissa first learned of his affair, she tried to scrape the stars off with a kitchen knife. Although Charles refused to confirm it, she suspected he and Chelsea had used the attic room on several occasions. She couldn't stand the thought of those stupid stars glowing down on them. But no matter how hard she scraped, the stars stuck fast. That would be a problem if they had to sell the house.

"No," she said out loud. She lay down on the yoga mat Charles had left on the floor and looked out the skylight at the few real stars that were visible. She loved this house, and without the house, there was no hope at all for her and Charles. But as far as she could see, there was only one way now to keep it.

Arthur Salvatore. He owned, coincidentally, a chocolate factory, though not the one Charles and his Grade One class would be visiting tomorrow. Boutique chocolates, rather than corner store. Melissa had submitted a bid on a project to promote a new line of exotic treats including chocolate-dipped scorpions and candied canary eggs. He usually awarded such contracts to bigger agencies, but when Mr. Salvatore saw Melissa's photo on her website, he called her personally.

"My dear, do you believe in fate?" he asked her. "I saw you last week at the opening of the new arts centre. We locked eyes across the crowded room, but when I tried to reach your side, you had vanished. Now I see I've been given another chance."

It must have been Chelsea he'd locked eyes with, Melissa realized, but she didn't tell him that. She agreed to meet him for lunch at a very expensive seafood restaurant in Yorkville. Normally, she would have picked up the tab, since she was trying to woo him as a client. But Arthur made it very clear that it was not merely a business lunch. "I intend to treat you like a lady," Arthur said. "I'm old fashioned."

You're old, Melissa thought. She was curious and frightened as he ran his hand up her thigh under the table. The contract he was offering would pay the mortgage and a lot more for the foreseeable future, but it was clear that her end of the bargain involved more than a promotional campaign. "Think about it, Missy," Arthur said. "I'll be in touch." Melissa hated being called Missy.

Chelsea wouldn't have hesitated for a moment. She'd always been the bold and daring one, ready and willing to disregard the rules and collateral damage in pursuit of her own selfish ends. Yet everyone continued to adore her, while Melissa, the cautious caretaker, was left cheated and on the verge of bankruptcy. She'd always resented and condemned Chelsea's behaviour, but now she found herself wishing she were more like her twin. If she only had such a brash and courageous soul, she'd have the nerve to do what it took to save her home.

She did feel very strange, hot and cold by turns, dizzy, and slightly nauseated. Was it possible that Charles was right? That she was experiencing a walk-in? That events were being orchestrated at a higher level to ensure she fulfilled her incarnational goals? The stick-on stars started whirling around her and she seemed to be levitating, rising toward the skylight. *It's really happening*, she thought.

She smiled in a way she was sure her old soul had never allowed her to smile before, as she lifted her phone and called Arthur's number.

"Arthur," she drawled in a sexy new voice. "I want to thank you again for the lovely lunch. I enjoyed myself immensely."

"That's great, Missy," Arthur said. His voice sounded strained. "How are you?"

"Better than ever," she said. "I can't tell you how much I'm looking forward to working with you." And it was true, she was looking forward to it. For the first time in her life she felt confident, in control. Whoever her walk-in was, it had to be someone powerful. A Viking princess, perhaps—she'd been told she had Viking blood. "Shall we meet again tomorrow?"

"Just a sec—" Arthur coughed. Melissa could hear a hubbub of noise around him, a voice speaking over a PA system. *Was he at the hospital?*

"Arthur, are you there?"

"I'm here, Missy, but I think we'll have to postpone a day or two. Seems I have a touch of food poisoning."

"Food poisoning?" she said. The starry sky tilted around her and her stomach lurched.

"It was probably the scallops."

Bouncing Lessons

The following are the recommendations contained in the Final Report of the Special Commission of Inquiry into the events surrounding the so-called "Bouncy Castle Tragedy" that transpired on July 23, 2018 at the annual Pebble Beach County Fair:

1. Local authorities should undertake a public awareness campaign advising parents of the unsuitability of gowns and tiaras for recreational activities involving vigorous jumping. In fact, tiaras, with their sharp points, are so hazardous that the commission recommends they be banned for use by all save real princesses.

2. Air pressure inside inflatable portions of bouncy castles should be reduced to prevent a loud pop — mimicking the sound of a gunshot — in the event that the castle is accidentally punctured by a sharp object.

3. All public announcements should be reviewed by a committee of communications experts before broadcast over fairgrounds' loudspeakers to prevent the rapid spread of unfounded rumours, such as, "Gunman by the bouncy castle!"

4. The amusement ride known as the Cyclone should be equipped with an automatic shut-off mechanism so that riders are not left spinning indefinitely when the operator becomes spooked by a rumour of gunfire and leaves his or her post without authorization.

5. Mallets used in the popular carnival game known as Whack-a-Mole should be tethered by bungee cord to the carnival booth to prevent their use as weapons by panicked patrons converging on the fairgrounds' exit.

6. Bouncy castles should not be situated near pens housing livestock, since even distinguished, prize-winning pigs and cattle will succumb to herd mentality and trample any and all obstacles if sufficiently alarmed by a stampeding crowd of humans.

7. In addition to the requisite first-aid kit, every bouncy castle should come equipped with cattle prods, several bottles of medicinal brandy and a lawyer to mitigate damage in the wake of a similar tragedy.

8. To counter potentially regressive and undemocratic values promoted to children by bouncy castles, manufacturers are encouraged to design alternatives such as bouncy parliament buildings, bouncy banks and bouncy universities.

The Commission agrees that every child has a right to bounce. Therefore, it is incumbent upon parents and policy-makers to ensure the above recommendations are implemented without delay. A supplementary commission of inquiry will be convened to investigate the potential for harnessing the vast renewable energy source expended by bouncing children worldwide.

Fear and Dissembling

"It usually happens early in the night, about thirty minutes after I first fall asleep," I explained to my counsellor Stacy.

I told her how every attack is unique in some way, but my state — one of utter terror — is always the same. It seems to press down on me, trying to enter, often with an immense, physical weight on my body, crushing the breath from my lungs and immobilizing me. The fear begins in my heart and surges like electricity through all my limbs, so that even my toes and fingertips feel afraid. But the most powerful sensation, and the worst, is a terrible and insistent sense of *presence*.

"I can't hear or see anything, but I'm convinced that there's someone there," I said.

"A person?" Stacy asked.

"I don't know. In the Middle Ages, they attributed this kind of thing to demons," I said.

Stacy raised an eyebrow and shifted forward in her seat. I'm glad that she finds her job interesting. My own job is to put those little stickers on fruit — which is not exactly the most meaningful vocation. In fact, people can be quite insulting when they find out I'm responsible for the stickers, which are such a pain to remove, so I usually say I'm in labelling.

"Is that what you think is happening?" Stacy asked. "That you're being visited by a demon?"

Last night it stood at my feet so real and palpable in its presence that when I finally managed to shake off the paralysis I tried to kick it away, kicked so hard that I wrenched a muscle in my leg. For a few seconds, despite the dark, I saw something, and I knew what it was that I was seeing. But when I flicked on the lights and the terror subsided, so too did that moment of insight. It slipped from my mind's grasp and I no longer knew what moments earlier I had understood.

"I have no idea what it is. You're the professional. What do you think?"

"There are various theories about what causes this kind of sleep paralysis. There could be several contributing factors, usually related to stress," Stacy said. She suggested I keep a notebook by my bed to write down as much detail as possible about each attack as soon as it occurs, before I forget anything.

"Have you ever seen *The Nightmare* by the eighteenth-century Swiss painter Henry Fuseli?" I asked Stacy.

She shook her head.

The painting depicts a grotesque, leering creature squatted on the midriff of a beautiful woman fainted dead away on her bed—a precise depiction of my next attack. The terrifying sense of presence felt concentrated, as if a being, just like Fuseli's, was straddling my chest, although its weight greatly exceeded what seemed possible for its small size. I couldn't breathe and seriously feared my ribcage would be crushed.

It was traditionally thought that the intent of these demon visitations was not just to instil terror, but for sexual interference. A female demon, called a *succubus*, was blamed for attacking or seducing men; assaults on women were attributed to the demon's male counterpart, called *incubus*. Far from being presumed innocent, victims were suspected of complicity in these liaisons, or at the very least, deserving in some way of the attack.

"Do you think there could be a sexual component to my incubus attacks?" I asked.

"Do you feel aroused when it happens?"

"Not really. Just terrified, which is why I have trouble getting back to sleep."

"There you go."

"Mind you, I always have trouble sleeping after sex as well. I could be repressed. Isn't that what Freud would say?"

Stacy smiled. "I'm not a big proponent of Freud."

"Aren't you even going to ask me about my sex life?"

"Not unless you want to tell me."

"Nothing to tell. Not since my ex-husband and I broke up."

"You were married?"

"Technically, no. Which is why I have to live in a crummy basement apartment, while he gets to keep the house. Him and his new wife. Still, at least it's a walk-out basement —there's a door to the backyard right in my bedroom, which is convenient. And of course, I got to keep the cat. I like to focus on the positive things."

"I can see that," Stacy said.

She gave me a recording of ocean waves gently lapping the shore. The sound is supposed to soothe me back to sleep. She swears by it herself; says she doesn't fall asleep without it.

⚜

The next time, my incubus stood not at the foot of my bed, but at my left side. I posed the question to Stacy. "Why would it choose the left side of the bed?"

"What's on the right side?" she asked, sensibly, I suppose.

"The wall."

"There you go."

"But he's never been constrained by physical laws in the past. Why would a simple wall get in the way?"

"You seem convinced that these experiences are supernatural in origin," she said.

"Supernatural is a misnomer. It really just refers to natural phenomena we don't yet understand. Like ghosts."

"Do you believe in ghosts?" she asked.

"Doesn't everybody?"

"No," Stacy said.

"Ah, so they will say. But then they always have some little story of their own they can't explain. Like 'I don't believe in ghosts, but … once, when I was sitting at my desk, I heard my grandfather say my name as if he was right behind me, though I knew he was three hundred kilometres away. Later I learned he'd passed away at that very moment …' That kind of thing."

"Did that happen to you?"

"No. I was employing a hypothetical example. Everyone has some such story."

"I don't know about that," Stacy said. "But I do think this belief in the supernatural is adding to your fear, feeding the flames that prevent you from sleeping again after each episode. Alice, I don't doubt that you are having very fearful experiences. But maybe it's time for you to consider that what seems to be happening is not real."

⚜

Last night, when I first awoke, I was convinced for several seconds that my incubus was a giant raccoon sitting at the end of my bed. This is not entirely unprecedented. There are occasional reports of incubi appearing in animal form, though none specifically of raccoons. The most common form is of a large black dog.

"A raccoon," I said to Stacy. "What do you think that means?"

"Did you see a raccoon at some point during the day?"

"I see raccoons every day. In the back yard outside my bedroom window. Zeke, my cat, likes to sit and watch them descend from the trees at dusk. But that doesn't explain why my incubus appeared as one. What does Jung say about raccoons? Don't they have some kind of archetypal meaning?"

Stacy sighed ever so slightly. "Not everything has a meaning, Alice. Some things are just random. In the absence of meaning the brain sometimes grabs the nearest thing, an image or a pattern, to try to process what it experiences."

Nearly a week without a peep from my incubus, and then bam! He returned, and this time, he was wearing a puffy coat. In fact, there were several aspects of this visit that were different from the previous ones. First of all, it was much later, nearly three-thirty in the morning. Secondly, my incubus didn't stop or disappear into thin air. As soon as I opened my eyes and saw him, he turned and walked out of the bedroom. It occurred to me that maybe Puffy Coat was not my incubus, but a flesh and blood intruder.

I grabbed my telephone from my bedside table. If it was an intruder, I should call 9-1-1, I thought. But Stacy's words came back to me: *consider that it's not real.* If I called the police about what turned out to be just another incubus sighting, I might be charged with mischief, or worse — they could call in Stacy and admit me to the psych ward. Then who would take care of Zeke? I wasn't confident enough of the intruder's reality to call the police, nor was I sufficiently convinced of his incorporeality to risk walking into the next room where an intruder might still be lying in wait.

I weighed the likelihood of the two possibilities. If the intruder was real, how did he get in, and how did he get all the way to my bedroom without my hearing him and waking up? (I forgot, until much later, about the ocean waves.) Surely I would have heard something, or sensed his presence before he got so far. And if he was real, where was he now? Stacy was right. In this case, the incubus was the simpler, and therefore more likely explanation.

I opened my notebook and recorded all of the unique

aspects of this particular attack, then I managed to sleep until my alarm went off and I woke up nearly freezing cold. When I went into the living room, I understood why: the front window was broken, the glass shattered on the floor. My purse was gone.

⚜

"You were wrong!" I said to Stacy at my appointment two days later. "It *was* real!"

"Alice, you must realize that this break-in has nothing to do with the night terrors you've been experiencing," Stacy said. "It's just a coincidence."

"Just a coincidence that's made me realize something very important."

"What is that?" Stacy asked.

"Which is worse: a visit from an incubus? Or a flesh and blood intruder? I mean, has anyone actually died of an incubus attack?"

Stacy frowned. "I couldn't say."

"If they did, it was probably a heart attack brought on by fear. Which means they weren't killed by an incubus, but by their response to an incubus."

"I'm not sure what this has to do—"

"Puffy Coat could have killed me, or at least caused me grave bodily harm. Don't you see what this means? It means there's no reason to be afraid of my incubus!"

"Alice, I appreciate your desire to look on the bright side, but there may be some more practical issues you should be focusing on. Like maybe you should consider putting bars on your windows."

"The police said the most important thing is to take precautions against identity theft, but I say, with my credit rating, Puffy Coat is welcome to my identity! I could do with a new one."

This made Stacy smile. A tight little mouth-only smile, but a smile nonetheless, before she started going on again about dissociation from reality. She just doesn't get it.

⚜

I was beginning to worry that my incubus had given up on me, that I'd taken too long to let go of my fear and lost my chance, but last night he returned. I heard a shuffling sound and could see a sort of murkiness at the foot of my bed. Even though I told myself over and over that I shouldn't be afraid, my body became petrified of its own accord. I had no control over it. It's like I'm allergic to incubi, or something, the way my ex was allergic to Zeke. The murkiness moved along the side of my bed and then it sat down. I saw the depression in the mattress. It was sitting right there beside me.

I kept telling myself don't be afraid, don't be afraid, but my body remained paralyzed with fear. I tried to move my hand toward it, not to touch it, but to make a gesture of acceptance, to let it know that I wasn't intentionally pushing it away. I concentrated all my attention on my hand. It was incredibly difficult keeping the fear at bay, but I managed to raise my pinkie finger, and bam! Just like that, it was gone. Disappeared. No more depression in the mattress, no murkiness, no sense of presence.

"Do you know what all angel visitations in the Bible have in common?" I asked Stacy. "The first thing the angel always says is 'Do not be afraid.' Mary, Zechariah, Paul, they were all terrified. But the angels weren't there to harm them. They were there to make them aware of their true callings. It's just that the body responds to the presence of danger the same way it does to the divine. The word fear has the same root as revere."

"Do you believe in God?" Stacy asked.

"As an old white man with a beard? No. But someone's got to be behind all this."

Thinking of old white men with beards gave me an idea. Maybe I needed to do something pro-active to encourage my incubus before he showed up and I became too scared to move. I decided to leave a glass of milk and some cookies for him on my bedside table. I wasn't sure what kind of cookie an incubus would prefer, so I chose a variety: jelly centred, chocolate digestive and vanilla cream. The first night I woke to the sound of gentle slurping and I thought, *yes, it worked*! But it was only Zeke lapping the milk. The cookies were untouched.

The next night I placed the plate of cookies on top of the milk glass so Zeke couldn't get at it. I had a prickly feel-ing as I went to sleep, as if my incubus was already in the vicinity, and sure enough, half an hour later, bam! I was wide awake again, my body paralyzed with fear. I could open my eyes, but I couldn't lift my head, for a great weight was holding me down. Then slowly but surely, the blankets slithered down to the foot of my bed as if someone was standing there pulling them away. I tried to speak, to draw attention to the friendly snack I'd left, but I couldn't even move my jaw. I don't know how long I lay like that before it was just suddenly gone. I admit, I felt so shaken at first that I ate the cookies myself. But once I calmed down and thought about it a bit, I realized that the covers pulled away represented a breakthrough. My incubus had spoken in metaphor: the truth was about to be revealed.

That same day, just before noon, the police called to say they had a suspect in custody and did I think I could pick him out of a line-up. Though she tried to hide it, I could tell Stacy was impressed by this development.

"Were you able to identify your intruder?" she asked.

"I wasn't sure at first," I said. "They were all wearing puffy coats, and when they put their hoods up and turned to the side, they *looked* exactly the same. But I just knew which one was the right one. I could feel it."

Stacy looked alarmed. "You told the police that?"

"I just pointed to the right one, and told them I was certain."

Stacy coughed. "Alice, what sort of truth are you hoping to discover in all this?"

"I wanted to ask Puffy Coat how he knew which apartment to break into. Was he visited by an incubus who told him to do it, or was he just drawn subconsciously to my window?"

"You spoke to him?" Stacy asked.

"No. The police wouldn't let me. Which is outrageous, I mean, we've obviously got a cosmic connection."

I decided to try a savoury snack this time, some crackers with goat's cheese and sundried tomatoes, and mineral water instead of milk. I fell asleep quickly. When I awoke, the blankets had already been removed and whatever was standing at the foot of my bed was pulling off my socks. Like the previous night, I couldn't move; a huge weight seemed to be holding me down. I could see the murkiness again, swirling around my feet. Then my toes started to tingle, as if with pins-and-needles, and it seemed the cloud of murkiness was *entering my left foot*. It spread through the veins of my leg, then throughout my entire body, to the tips of my fingers and top of my head. When the whole cloud had disappeared inside me, I fell instantly back to sleep.

What is more unnerving than discovering someone has been reading your journal, is realizing someone else has been writing it—the ultimate identity theft. All I could remember about last night was the smell of goat's cheese as I drifted off to sleep. I did wonder why my feet were bare when I got up, since I always wear socks to bed, but I also felt well-rested and energized, as I hadn't been in a very long time. I even noticed a new sparkle in my eye, as I looked in the mirror and brushed my teeth, a certain glow to my complexion. Only when I opened up my notebook, did I find the above explanation, in my own handwriting no less.

"Do you think you could hypnotize me?" I asked Stacy. "To recover the lost memory?"

Stacy frowned. I wonder how satisfying she is finding her job these days. "Alice, I'm concerned," she said. "The trauma of the break-in you experienced might be affecting you more than you realize. Sometimes our psyches block understanding to protect us."

I laughed, because it's so obvious that I am *more* perceptive than most people. I actually possess a remarkable acuity when it comes to ferreting out hidden connections to discover the truth.

⚜

The following week Stacy asked whether I was still experiencing incubus attacks.

"Of course not," I said. "My incubus doesn't need to visit me anymore. He's always with me. He's part of me now. You're getting paid to listen to me, remember?" I really shouldn't have to tell her how to do her job.

"And how is your job going?" she asked.

"I quit. I always sensed that I was meant for something greater than stickering fruit. Now my incubus has inspired me live up to it. "

"Do you think that's wise? To quit before you have another job lined up?"

"I'm thinking I'll work as a police consultant, on some of their difficult cases."

"Is that realistic?"

I feel sorry for Stacy. She has such a limited understanding of reality. "The police called me again," I told her. "They recovered my ID from a locker to which Puffy Coat had the key."

Stacy's eyebrows flew up. "You mean the man you identified in the line-up?"

"Of course," I said. I don't know why she was so surprised.

"Did you get anything else back? Your purse?"

"No. And I told the police I didn't really need the ID

back either. Biblical figures often changed their names after being visited by angels: Abram became Abraham, Jacob became Israel, Saul became Paul. So I'm going to do the same. After all, I'm really not the same person anymore, am I? What do you think of Anastasia?"

The police declined to use my services. Perhaps they will reconsider once my reputation is more established. I did convince them to accept one of the cards I had made up with my company name: Answers from Anastasia. Sounds much better than Answers from Alice.

There is no need to tell Stacy of this development. It doesn't change anything. It only makes my true vocation even clearer. I'm not being called to merely help the police track down petty thieves. No, there's something much bigger, more spectacular required of me, something to demonstrate that I am indeed real.

I trust my incubus will give me a sign.

It was so obvious it made me laugh. Stacy apologized in advance for keeping her phone on, explaining that she was expecting a crucial call from her mother's nursing home. When the call came, she slipped into the hall and closed the door. There it was, her purse, wide open in front of me, her wallet in clear view. My fingers tingled, this time with delight, as I extracted her driver's licence and slipped it into my sock. When she returned, she was none the wiser.

From there it couldn't have been easier to Google her address and find her house. It was a modest split-level in a suburban neighbourhood; ticky-tacky houses, with ticky-tacky locks. I waited until the last light was switched off, gave her some time to fall asleep, then waited another thirty minutes before I let myself in. I didn't even have to break a window; the one at the back of the garage just slid right open. Then I pried open the door between the garage and kitchen using Stacy's driver's licence to slide the bolt aside.

There was thick carpeting on the stairs to muffle my footsteps as I crept up, though it was hardly necessary, as I could hear the roar of the ocean waves from down the hall. I traced the sound to her bedroom, and there she was, fast asleep. I watched her for a while, but she didn't wake, not until I climbed on the bed and straddled her torso, my knees on her arms and my hand over her mouth. When her eyes flew open, I gave her a few moments to see me, to adjust to reality, to comprehend. I removed my puffy coat and held it over her face while she struggled, until she stopped.

Natural Selection

In 2016, scientists were excited by the discovery of a previously unclassified species of rodent inhabiting some remote areas of southern Saskatchewan. At first glance, these creatures appear to be closely related to the common prairie gopher, but further study has revealed some significant and surprising differences. Unlike other rodents, and in fact most mammals, save great apes and humans, these gophers have no tails.

"It is possible that the missing tail was initially a genetic accident that became common to the population through intense inbreeding," says Dr. Arbuthnot, head of the laboratory studying the gophers. But observation of the rodents' behaviour has led some members of Dr. Arbuthnot's team to speculate whether tail-lessness evolved in the species to favour advantageous behaviour, the same way tail-lessness in homo sapiens facilitated the ability to walk upright. These gophers do not generally walk on two legs, but they do spend a remarkable amount of time seated upright with their hind legs folded into the lotus position, something a tail would certainly prohibit. Beginning when they are just a few weeks old, the gophers adopt this position and hold it for anywhere from thirty to ninety minutes several times a day. Monitors show that their heart rates slow to between fifty and one hundred beats per minute while in this position, less than a quarter of the rate during normal rest.

"This drastic slowdown of breathing and heart rates is unheard of even in hibernating animals," says Dr. Arbuthnot.

The only comparable results, as research by some of Dr. Arbuthnot's colleagues reveals, have been obtained in tests carried out on Tibetan monks as they meditate.

"Of course, we cannot prove that these gophers are actually meditating," says Arnold Salaam, a Ph.D. candidate working in Dr. Arbuthnot's lab. "It is simply the best analogy we have at present to describe their behaviour."

It was Salaam who subsequently discovered the gophers' apparent observation of the fast during Ramadan. "At first I thought they were sick. I put the food and water in their cages at about nine o'clock in the morning, as usual, but they refused to touch it and continued to abstain all day. I returned the next morning to find they'd consumed everything overnight. It took me a few days to make the connection," says Salaam, who is an observant Muslim himself. "Then I started coming in extra early to serve them breakfast before sunup. They appreciated that."

More remarkable than this celebration of Ramadan is the gophers' ability to discern the precise moments of sunup and sundown without benefit of clocks or windows by which to observe the skies. "It's as if they have a sixth sense," says animal behaviourist Angela Miskin, "a sense of religion."

The laboratory team has conducted a number of experiments proving that the *Marmota spiritus*, as the species has now been officially named, consistently favour consecrated communion wafers over non-consecrated ones when given the choice of a snack. They also refuse to urinate on shredded pages torn from the Bible, the Koran or the Bhagavad Gita; no such scruples are shown to newspapers, detective fiction, or classics of Canadian literature. While the *Marmota spiritus* enjoy gnawing on plastic figurines of Mickey Mouse and Spiderman, they treat similarly sized statues of Buddha and Ganesh with reverence, setting them up on flat stones with offerings of fresh grubs. On Christmas morning, the scientists all rushed to the lab to witness the animals exchanging small gifts crafted from twigs and mud.

"It is much too early to say definitively that we have discovered the first species — aside from humans — of religious animals," says Dr. Arbuthnot.

The implications are reverberating around the world nonetheless.

"This is great news for ecumenical and interfaith peace efforts," says religious scholar Helen Minelli. "How appropriate that we should find role models among God's most humble creatures."

Famous atheist Harold Hawkins, on the other hand, warns: "These fanatical rodents should be rounded up and interrogated. They may be harbouring terrorist cells."

Securing funds to conduct ongoing research on these fascinating animals has become a delicate political process, but scientists at the lab are determined to continue even if it means volunteering their own time and resources.

"The work gets more exciting every day," says Angela

Miskin. Tests are currently being carried out on apparent stigmata—spontaneous bleeding from all four paws—on one of the more charismatic of the *Marmota spiritus* in the colony. "Results so far are inconclusive," Miskin adds, "but I'm not ruling out a miracle."

The Revelation to Keith

There would have been nothing out of the ordinary when Natasha whacked Keith with her biology textbook if he hadn't turned his head at the same moment she took her swing. Everyone whacked Keith on the way out of biology class. It was his punishment for always knowing more than everyone else, including the teacher. Even the teacher whacked him. Keith should have known to stay safely facing his locker while the blows rained down on the back of his head and his shoulders and butt.

"He did it on purpose," Natasha complained afterward. "He looked straight at me with his right eye and turned so suddenly, I didn't have a chance to stop. It's not fair."

Natasha's textbook caught Keith full across the face, cracking the right lens of his pop-bottle-bottom glasses in a zigzag line. Keith's back slid down his locker until his bottom hit the floor; his legs splayed in front of him and his eyes popped wide open in a daze. He remained this way for three days.

The paramedics managed to ease his body into a more

comfortable position on a stretcher and subsequently a hospital bed, but nobody, not the nurses, the attending physician, nor the ophthalmologist on call could close his eyes. The lids would slide down pliably enough, only to pop immediately back open. Even a mortician was called in to give it a whirl, without success. "This is why they used to place coins on the eyes of the dead," he said.

But Keith was far from dead. His breathing and pulse were strong, and magnetic resonance imaging recorded brain activity that was off the charts. His mother tried playing his favourite Mahler symphonies, and his father tried reading out the most challenging calculus proofs he could find, to no avail. Keith gave no sign of seeing or responding to anyone. There was nothing to do but lubricate his eyes with drops every fifteen minutes and wait.

On the third day, at exactly 6:30 a.m., Keith blinked and asked if he could have eggs for breakfast. Mid-morning his ophthalmologist Dr. Carson entered the room.

"I understand your mother brought in a spare pair of your glasses?" he asked.

"Yes. But I don't need them anymore," Keith said. "I'm no longer farsighted. My vision is perfect. In fact, I am now *deep*-sighted."

"Deep-sighted?"

"I see things as they *really* are."

"I see," Dr. Carson said.

"I doubt it."

Dr. Carson cleared his throat. He patted the pockets of his white coat before removing a small device which he pointed at the wall, projecting an eye chart. "Read out the smallest line you can see clearly."

"S-e-c-o-n-d-c-o-m-i-n-g," Keith read.

Dr. Carson coughed again and examined Keith's file. "It says here that you've suffered from migraines for several years."

"Yes. Since infancy. Always the right side of my head."

"And were these ever preceded by visual distortions?"

"Not distortions. Clarifications breaking through, hints of the big one to come," Keith explained.

"So you would describe this latest episode as the big one?"

"You're not kidding. Road to Damascus."

Dr. Carson nodded thoughtfully. "Where are your parents, did they go home?"

"I believe they are in the cafeteria."

The door opened. "Natasha," Keith said, even before her wary face appeared.

"This your girlfriend?" Dr. Carson asked.

Natasha's eyes widened in horror. "I'm not his girlfriend! Gawd! I'm his bully."

"Well, then I'm sure you have a lot to talk about," Dr. Carson said, taking Keith's file with him as he hurried out of the room. Natasha watched him leave with an expression that suggested he smelled very bad.

"Thanks for coming, Natasha," Keith said.

She shrugged. "My dad said I had to. He took away my iPhone until I did." She avoided Keith's gaze, looking lingeringly at the walls instead as if they were covered with great art, and she was actually interested in art.

"How have you been?" Keith asked.

"I got suspended for three days, you know. It's not fair. Sam Crawford hit you much harder than I did. I saw him. And he didn't get punished at all."

"I know. I remember," Keith said.

Natasha snuck a look at him. "Do you remember anything from when you were, you know, asleep?"

"I wasn't asleep. Quite the opposite, in fact. I was experiencing the reawakening of the bicameral mind."

Natasha blinked.

"Up until about 3,000 years ago, the human brain functioned very differently. Right brain and left brain operated independently. The left brain would hear what it perceived as voices from outside, that were in fact emanating from parts of the right brain that in most people are now dormant. Ancient peoples interpreted these as the voices of gods. When you hit me, it triggered the full reawakening of my right brain."

"I didn't do it on purpose," Natasha said.

"Actually, that's *exactly* what you did. You just don't realize it because your right brain is still asleep. But don't worry. I'm only exceptional in the sense that I'm on the cusp of this momentous change. It's the next leap of human evolution. Soon we'll all hear the voices of the gods again, even you."

"You hear voices?" Natasha glanced at the door as if to map out an escape.

"Unlike the ancients, my fully functioning right brain is matched by the dazzling analytic and computational skill that developed in modernity in the left hemisphere. While I can 'hear' what my right brain is saying, I am aware that the voices are in fact thoughts emanating from within. The mind of God is right here." Keith tapped his right temple.

"So, what, you're like Jesus or something?"

"Jesus would be a good analogy, yes."

"If you're God or Jesus, or whatever, how come you couldn't stop us all bullying you?"

"Jesus was bullied too."

"Gawd! We didn't exactly crucify you. It was just a couple of whacks!"

Keith patted the air, as if to calm Natasha down. "My point is, now that I can see the hidden reality of everything, now that I can hear the voice of God, I am aware that everything happens exactly as it is supposed to. There are no accidents. For example, Judas was always meant to betray Jesus with a kiss."

"No way am I going to kiss you," Natasha said. "Even if I never get my iPhone back."

"But don't you see?" Keith said. "Judas had to do it. He actually sacrificed himself and his reputation for all time to play that necessary role. Just as you played an essential role in my reawakening by whacking me in the head. So thank you. I hope you can appreciate that your current suffering is part of a greater good."

The profound truth of this insight pierced Natasha to the heart. She had always been keenly aware of the hidden order that reigned in the classroom and on the playground. Sure, she felt sorry for the kids she'd teased or allowed to plummet to the pavement when she jumped off the teeter-totter. But she realized now that she didn't have a choice. Why else would she have been born so pretty? All along, something inside her had been telling her exactly what she had to do to take her proper place in the universe, even if it resulted in suffering. Tears sprang to her eyes as she looked down at her pink platform sandals.

"I missed a French test because of the suspension. They'll probably fail me," she said.

"I could help you make it up," Keith said. "When they let me out of here."

Natasha looked up. "Would you?" She took a step towards the bed just as the room door flew open, smacking her in the forehead and knocking her against the wall. Keith's parents rushed in followed by Dr. Carson, the attending psychiatrist Dr. Aziz, and two other unidentified white-coats just in time to see Natasha slide down the wall until her bottom hit the floor. Her legs splayed in front of her and her eyes popped wide open in a daze.

Random Swerves

2:00 Perimeter foot check. Senior Security Officer Agnes Cardinal notes suspicious gathering of subjects in black unitards adjacent to front entrance, explains to Junior Security Trainee Will Tripp that the Museum of Incarceration is a frequent target for demonstrators. "Kooks and artists of all kinds," she says. The unitards unfurl a banner reading *Lucretius' Free Radicals.* "Lucretius," Trainee Tripp says, "Wasn't he a character on *The Addams Family*?" Officer Cardinal rolls her eyes then corrects trainee's patrol posture, noting tendency to slouch.

12:30 Key inventory. Officer Cardinal verbally conveys secret combination for safe containing museum keys to Trainee Tripp for memorization. "Say that again?" says Trainee Tripp, whipping out his smartphone. "I said mem-or-ize. Capiche?" says Officer Cardinal, repeats code eight times before trainee catches on. Notes trainee's subsequent inability to operate lock without reciting combination aloud.

13:00 Video surveillance review. "Meet SAM," says Officer Cardinal, indicating the main computer terminal and bank of CCTV screens. "Short for Suspicious Activity Monitoring. SAM is the most sophisticated security software on the market, capable of detecting the slightest aberration caught by any one of the museum's twenty-eight cameras." Trainee Tripp glances over his shoulder then back at the screens. "Hey! I can see myself!"

13:13 SAM detects aberrant behaviour pattern at museum front entrance triggering alarm. Officer Cardinal notes trainee's tendency to jump out of his skin at any loud noise. Front entrance camera CCTV check reveals seven subjects in black unitards playing Twister.

13:19 Front entrance foot check. No sign of offending unitards, only Twister mat with *The highest goal of civilization is the enhancement of pleasure* scrawled in green marker. Officer Cardinal snorts. "The only thing close to pleasure we can count on in this life is a sense of order. Everyone in their proper place, living the lives we were meant to live. Even Lucretius knew that. He said that civilization is the result of man's craving for security. Security. Safety. Knowing we won't be murdered in our beds by marauding terrorists. Do you know what that means?" Trainee Tripp shakes his head. "I guess I missed that episode." Officer Cardinal continues. "It means this museum represents the *height* of civilization!"

14:00 Upper body restraint room. Officer Cardinal instructs Trainee Tripp in the history of straitjackets, belly chains and all manner of manacles. "This display is a perfect metaphor for the human condition. Take the classic police handcuff." She snaps the cuffs on trainee's wrists before he realizes what is happening. "The more you struggle, the tighter they get," she says. Trainee Tripp tries to pull his hands out of the cuffs. "Ow!" he says. He tries again. "OW!" Officer Cardinal chuckles and removes cuffs.

14:13 SAM detects aberrant behaviour pattern triggering alarm. West corner exit camera CCTV check reveals seven subjects in black unitards doing the chicken dance. Trainee Tripp points at the screen and guffaws. Officer Cardinal notes trainee's lack of gravitas.

14:21 West corner foot check. No sign of offending unitards. Message scrawled in chalk on sidewalk reads, *The greatest obstacle to pleasure is not pain, but delusion.* Officer Cardinal snorts. "I'd like to see some of our little ballerinas subjected to life on the inside for a few days. Then ask them how they define the opposite of pleasure." Trainee Tripp nods, rubs his sore wrists.

15:00 Security devices room. Officer Cardinal instructs Trainee Tripp in the evolution and use of prisoner prods from sharp sticks to pepper spray and modern tasers. "If I were to taser Chief Unitard out there, he would experience pain equivalent to a thousand fish hooks piercing his skin from the inside." "Cool," says Trainee Tripp. "Lucretius does have a point about delusion, though," Officer Cardinal says. "When I was young I fantasized about being a prison guard, working my way up through the system to become warden. But with this club foot, it was never going to happen. I had to drop that delusion. Only then did I realize *this* was the job I was born to do. This museum is crucial to maintaining order and security, because it reassures the non-prison public. They can understand exactly how incarceration works without being exposed to the danger of an operational prison. It's my role to keep it safe, guard it from thieves and vandals. Once I realized that, everything became clear. I never got married, never had children, because I knew it would interfere with the night shifts. Been here thirty-two years now." Trainee Tripp whistles. "Wow. I'm just here temporarily, till I get my big break. I'm actually an actor." Officer Cardinal laughs so hard she forgets to make note of trainee's lack of commitment.

15:13 SAM detects aberrant behaviour pattern triggering alarm. East corner exit camera CCTV check reveals seven subjects in black unitards tossing wet noodles at each other.

15:18 East corner foot check. No sign of offending unitards. Message spelled out in alphabet pasta reads, *The random swerve of particles is the basis of free will.* "Free will—hah!" Officer Cardinal notes. "Now there's a delusion for you." Trainee Tripp nudges pasta with his foot, asks: "When do I get a dinner break?"

16:00 Lower body restraint room. Officer Cardinal instructs Trainee Tripp in the history of leg irons, shackles, and balls-and-chains. "What kind of people do you think ended up here in these chains?" she asks. Trainee Tripp looks thoughtful. "Criminals and psychopaths?" he says. "And do you think it is by anything but the grace of God that you weren't born a psychopath fated to become a killer or a bank robber?" Officer Cardinal shouts. Trainee Tripp blushes. "I did steal gummy bears from the corner store once, but I went back and apologized." Officer Cardinal makes a note to double check trainee's criminal record.

16:13 SAM detects aberrant behaviour pattern triggering alarm. Back exit camera CCTV check reveals seven subjects in black unitards performing a group hug.

16:20 Back exit foot check. No sign of offending unitards. Large red cardboard heart contains message reading, *Death is nothing but the liberation of particles. There is no afterlife.* Officer Cardinal snorts. "No afterlife—they wish! There is so an afterlife, and let me tell you, it's as miserable as this one." "I'm hearing that you need a hug," says Trainee Tripp. Officer Cardinal mutters: "I'm hearing that you need a hearing aid."

17:00 Prisoner interrogation techniques room. Officer Cardinal instructs Trainee Tripp on the evolution of torture from the rack to waterboarding. "Did people actually die here?" Trainee Tripp asks. Officer Cardinal scoffs. "There's not a square foot on earth where someone hasn't been murdered. And the sorry fools who succumbed to torture here are all the proof you need of an afterlife. I still hear their screams and groans sometimes. You will too." Trainee Tripp turns white.

17:13 Security system detects perimeter breach triggering alarm. Officer Cardinal suggests they split up to locate intruders. Trainee Tripp asks if he can take a taser. "You could, but it won't do you any good. They've been decommissioned," says Officer Cardinal. "De-what?" he asks. "No batteries," she replies. Each takes a standard baton instead and they head in opposite directions.

17:29 Prison clothing room. Officer Cardinal notes store of striped prison pyjamas has been ransacked, but no other sign of intruders. Hears screams from other side of museum.

17:34 Restraining furniture room. Officer Cardinal finds Trainee Tripp strapped into Devil's Chair. "They threw marshmallows at me!" he says. Evidence of alleged marshmallow assault litters floor. Officer Cardinal frees trainee from restraints, notes that he has been crying. "Did you see which way they went?" she asks. Trainee Tripp points to the stairs.

17:41 Museum roof exit. Officer Cardinal and Trainee Tripp emerge from the open door cautiously. No sign of offending unitards, only a pair of wind-up teeth chattering in a circle. "Careful, it might be booby-trapped," warns Officer Cardinal as they approach. The teeth slow down their chattering and come to a stop. As Officer Cardinal pokes the teeth with her baton, seven subjects now wearing old-fashioned striped prison pyjamas over their unitards jump out from behind a smokestack and necklace her and Trainee Tripp with fat inner tubes. They pull the inner tubes down over their torsos so that their arms are trapped against their sides. The seven then form a ring, sing "Born Free" while gently pushing their prisoners into the centre where their inner tubes collide and bounce randomly.

17:49 Chief unitard points to the sky and shouts: "Here it comes!" He and his co-conspirators whoop and clap as a yellow hot-air balloon with a smiley face on it descends to the museum roof. Its sole occupant, a young woman in a unitard and wizard hat tosses out ropes for the others to hold the balloon's basket in place on the roof while the balloon stays aloft. The wizard jumps out, does eenie-meenie-mynie-mo between the two prisoners, settling on Officer Cardinal, who is subsequently lifted and heaved into the balloon basket.

17:57 Officer Cardinal's life flashes before her eyes, from five-year-old Agnes trapping her little brother in an upside down playpen to play prison guard, to just last week when she reported her mother's nursing home grow-op to police. For the first time in her life, she experiences regret.

18:00 The wizard yanks the inner tube up, freeing Officer Cardinal's arms, just as the co-conspirators begin letting out rope, allowing the balloon to rise. Looking down from the basket as Trainee Tripp grows smaller and smaller, Officer Cardinal experiences an unfamiliar maternal twinge. She is relieved to see his captors remove the shackling inner tube, but relief turns to horror as he removes his security guard uniform to reveal the black unitard beneath.

Assurance of Things Hoped For

ello?

—Hello, Mrs. Grantham?

—Yes?

—Mrs. Grantham! How are you this evening?

—Fine. Who is this?

—Fantastic. My name is Logan. But pleasantries aside, Mrs. Grantham, how are you *really* this evening?

—What?

—Do you feel that your life has meaning?

—Who is this?

—Logan. As I said. I'm calling tonight to tell you about a new product that will give you and your family a sense of peace and security regardless of the crises you may face down the road.

—I've already got life insurance.

—I'm not talking about the mere fact of biological life. I'm talking about something that in the grand scheme of things is far more important. I'm talking about Faith Insurance.

—Faith Insurance?

—You hear the stories all the time, don't you? Sad, tragic stories of people losing their faith at precisely the moment they need it most, moments of pain or failure or stress brought on by dramatic changes. We are offering a new and innovative product that will protect you and your family from just such a tragedy. It's called the Job Policy—as in the Book of Job. By which we do not mean to privilege faiths of the Judeo-Christian sort. Job symbolically, you understand, as a story of a man whose faith survived even the greatest calamity and intellectual challenges. In fact, we provide coverage for faiths of all kinds. There are the organized religions, of course: Jainism, Hinduism, Zoroastrianism—you name it, we've got it covered. We also cover people in categories of non-organizational faith, like Unitarians, New Agers, or the "spiritual but not religious." Let me ask you, Mrs. Grantham, do you ascribe to a particular faith?

—I was brought up Presbyterian.

—Aaaaaahhh! I'm afraid that puts you at very high risk. Are you aware that since 1980 membership in Presbyterian churches has dropped by 85%?

—I think some of those members likely died—

—Which makes it all the more tragic. Imagine dying without the comfort of one's faith.

—I don't see how insurance—

—The process could not be simpler. You will need to provide a full faith history describing your current status and any previous lapses or conversions. The forms can be downloaded from our website www.meaningforlife.com. Once it is endorsed by appropriate clergy we will provide you with a quote. Prices range depending on the level of risk assessed, but I can tell you it is only the most hardened of sceptics — professional atheists, for example, or tax auditors — who are denied coverage.

— Look, we don't have a lot of extra money to be spending these days.

— Mrs. Grantham, this is not about money. There are plenty of insurance policies out there that will guarantee your financial security or pay for a university education. But what good are those things if your life has no meaning?

— I have three children. My life has plenty of meaning.

— Children provide imperative while they're young, Mrs. Grantham, but that's not the same as meaning. What happens when they leave home? When you and your spouse are left with an empty nest? Maybe you'll develop an online gambling addiction. Or perhaps your husband will have an affair.

— I beg your pardon!

— No reason to be ashamed, Mrs. Grantham. When life is leached of meaning, these things are bound to happen to the best of us. But that's why I'm calling you tonight! By guaranteeing your faith, we can help you cope with these kinds of mid-life crises! Or any-time-of-life-crises. The only circumstances through which your faith cannot be ensured by our policies are the apocalypse and a mass invasion from outer space. Mrs. Grantham, if you purchase a full family policy, your spouse will be covered, as will your children up until age thirty — because, let's face it, thirty is the new nineteen. After thirty, they're on their own.

— We're in the middle of supper here —

—Ah! So tell me, did you remember to say grace before you began to eat?

—Well, no—

—Your faith is slipping already. It's crucial that you get insurance before it's too late. And if you buy now, you'll also receive a set of twelve steak knives with genuine olive wood handles carved in the shape of Jesus' disciples. Judas Iscariot has an extra long blade.

—I'd have to think about it.

—What's to think about? There's no call for complex calculation when your immortal soul is at stake. This is faith we're talking about, not taxes. As Søren Kierkegaard said: "Faith begins where thinking leaves off."

—But I'd at least have to speak to my husband first.

—Why not surprise him? What better way to say "I love you" than to save his eternal life?

—That's hardly—

—The truth is, Mrs. G, it's not just your family's souls you'd be insuring, but mine as well. You see, my own wife left me.

—I'm sorry to hear that—

—Then my car was totalled, my online ID was hacked and used to purchase a truckload of lady's lingerie—I'm still fighting that one in court—and to top it all off, last week my entire collection of exotic fish died. Some kind of tropical fish SARS, apparently.

—I just don't see—

—Mrs. G, this job is all I've got left. If I'm let go, I have nothing left to live for.

—What about your faith? I'm assuming it's insured.

—I'm still on probation here. I won't be eligible for the

company plan for another two weeks, so of course, if I get fired tonight ... Mrs. G, you don't want to be responsible for condemning my soul to the everlasting perdition of meaninglessness, do you?

—Of course not—

—So how would you like to pay?

By Grace

Gloria is just settling back into her mahogany French rococo chaise lounge with a large gin and tonic, when a knock at the door startles her. The servants were instructed not to disturb her. Visitors have to check in with the guards at the front gate, and she can always see their approach on security monitors several minutes in advance.

"Who is it?" she calls sharply.

"It's me," says a familiar voice as the door opens.

Gloria sits upright. She hasn't seen Lucifer since she was sixteen years old. On that occasion, he didn't bother to knock first. He simply materialized behind her, as she peered into the mirror of her improvised dressing table. It was really just a desk with a mirror propped against the wall, but she'd duct-taped a string of Christmas lights around the frame to make it look more like the dressing rooms of stars she'd seen in movies. She'd been gazing at her visage for over an hour, trying to find the most alluring expression and pose, while contemplating her dilemma: When would she finally be discovered? Stardom seemed so distant from the dead-end town of Humphrey, and her family's pig farm that was always on the brink of bankruptcy. "I would give anything to be famous," she'd murmured, and it was at that moment the Angel of Darkness appeared.

"That can be arranged," he'd said.

Shivers had circled the young Gloria's scalp; she'd felt afraid, but she was also a little thrilled. He was, after all, a very handsome man.

Forty years on, Lucifer is as sleek and debonair as ever.

At sixteen Gloria had the sense to stipulate that her fame be accompanied by great wealth before she agreed to a deal; if only she'd also thought to specify that she always remain thin. At the moment, she is in one of her plumper stages; she adjusts her muumuu self-consciously as she stands to greet her old friend. But when she sees what he is carrying, she gasps. "Why did you bring that?"

After her teenage self had signed her name in blood — he had nicked the inside of her elbow with an expert flick of a polished nail — he'd leaned in so close to her face, that Gloria thought he was about to kiss her. Instead, he'd made a soft sucking sound that grew to a rushing wind as her soul, sparkling like her lit-up mirror, emerged from her mouth and nose. It swirled once around the room before slithering into the clear glass bottle Lucifer holds before her now. Gloria had been surprised that her soul fit in such a small container; it was the size of a bottle of Tabasco sauce, and was stoppered with a miniature cork.

Lucifer sighs. "There was a clerical error. Turns out you are one of the elect."

"That can't be!"

"It's true. Chosen before the foundations of the world were laid. Our deal is null and void," he explains.

"But what does that mean for all this?" Gloria sweeps her arm around the room. "What about my career?"

Wealth magazine recently ranked Gloria the fourth richest celebrity in North America. She is queen of an empire, anchored by her top-rated talk show *Gloria!* into the homes of her fans through every possible medium: material, digital, and possibly even subliminal. There are movies, magazines, a line of designer hoodies-for-foodies (i.e. plus size), and a patented weight-loss programme all of which bear her signature, with a cute little trident for an i. Her monthly Positive Thinkers Club features gurus, authors and entrepreneurs who've changed their lives by changing their minds —and reaped a lot of money in the process. Adoring fans around the world chant mantras and leave themselves encouraging Post-its around their homes and offices in the hopes that they too can tap into the magic.

"There'll be some kind of fall from grace—forgive the pun. A scandal of some kind, I suppose. Sweatshops full of children maybe, or charges for tax evasion. Whatever the means, you'll lose everything. And I wouldn't rule out jail time."

"Jail!" Gloria wails. "But I've worked hard for all this. I climbed my way up from small town beginnings—"

"Gloria, Gloria," Lucifer chuckles and shakes his head. "You may be able to foist that nonsense on the millions of pathetic housewives tuning in for their Gloria fix every day at four o'clock, but you can't fool me. All that positive thinking crap! You and I both know the truth about your big break. Who do you think gave old farmer Fergus laryngitis?"

Young Gloria had stepped in at the last minute when Fergus O'Gammy, legendary host of *Lives-Talk*, a local radio call-in show about farm animals, was suddenly struck mute by a mysterious throat bug. Gloria, who'd been working Saturdays for a cleaning company, was emptying the station's wastebaskets when she became aware of the producer's plight. When she informed him that she lived on a pig farm, she was rushed into the studio and the host's chair where she turned on her voluminous charm for the farmers of southern Ontario. She never looked back.

"That was just the beginning—"

"Who do you think misfiled your competitors' applications to make sure you got your own cable station?" Lucifer says. "If it wasn't for me your fans would be improving their minds with the Algebra Channel, instead of being deluded into believing that if they say 'I am a success' to themselves in the mirror each morning they will make it so."

"Self-esteem is very important—"

"And who do you think ruined all those ballots to make sure you won an Emmy? I could go on."

"I resent that!" Gloria stamps her foot. "Maybe I have had a few strokes of luck, but I've also worked like a maniac for all this. I'm up at five-thirty every morning and I rarely get to bed before midnight."

"So does your housekeeper Connie. What does she have? A damp bachelor apartment in your basement and bunions I wouldn't care to inflict, even on a saint."

Gloria pouts for a few moments before changing tack. "So what about Connie? What's going to happen to her, when I lose my fortune? She'll be out of a job and have no place to live."

"Ah, concern for the poor and meek!" Lucifer laughs. "You're revealing your true nature already."

"How do you know I wouldn't have achieved all this even if I hadn't signed over my soul?" Gloria asks. "I couldn't be where I am today without some inherent talent! I've earned this!"

"If you really believe that, Gloria, you won't be afraid to take this back," Lucifer says, holding out the bottle.

Gloria shrinks from the sight of the sparkling mist inside and sits down heavily on her chaise lounge. "I need another drink. Do you want one?"

"Please," Lucifer says, taking a seat opposite while setting the bottle down in front of him.

Gloria presses a discreet button on her side table. "How could this have happened — this clerical error?" she asked.

"It's St. Peter. He's been showing signs of dementia for centuries."

The door opens again and a tiny woman wearing a black uniform, white apron and heavy orthopaedic shoes enters the room. "Two martinis please, Connie," Gloria says.

Connie gives Lucifer only the smallest, nearly imperceptible glance before stepping silently to the bar. She mixes two martinis swiftly and expertly, then places them on the coffee table without a clink or a drop spilled, then leaves without a sound.

"Isn't she a gem? A silent little mouse who carries out my every whim," Gloria says. She takes a large gulp of her drink and sighs. "I don't understand this 'chosen before the foundations of the earth' thing."

"I don't pretend to fully understand it myself, even if I

am the Devil. I mean *justification by faith*? You've got to be kidding me!"

"That's just it. I don't have faith!" Gloria says.

"Oh, you will, honey, you will." Lucifer takes a large gulp of his drink. "You'll need it."

"And I really have no say in the matter? What about you? I thought you were supposed to be the Great Satan."

"Look, this predestination thing predates me," he says. He's beginning to look annoyed.

"So you're as much of a dupe as I am. A puppet. Someone else is pulling the strings. Maybe even *you* are one of the elect."

"No way!" Anger flashes through Lucifer's eyes as he slams his glass down, rises to his feet and begins to pace, cracking his knuckles like firecrackers. "Believe me, I am solely responsible for all the evil in the universe. Your measly media empire, peddling lies and false hopes, is nothing compared to the destruction I have wrought!"

He recalls that when God ordered him to bow down to Adam at the beginning of time, he disobeyed out of conviction: it was wrong to bow down to a lesser being, and the snivelling little human Adam was undoubtedly that. What had happened to the proud Lucifer, that defiant rebel? After millennia of meddling in the affairs of earth, he's become cynical and complacent. He's beginning to wonder what he's really doing here, what is the point of his existence? Sure, he can still wreak havoc—there are more people on the planet now than ever to mess with—but to what end? Is Gloria right, is he really just the cosmos' biggest dupe?

"You've got to take control," Gloria says. "What would happen if you disobeyed, kept my soul?"

They both shift their gaze to the bottle on the table. The tiny cloud inside seems to be swirling faster. The truth is, Lucifer has no idea what will happen.

"You revolted once before," Gloria says. "Why not do it again? I would, if I were you. I would fight for my empire, no matter what the Bible says."

"But say I do revolt again," Lucifer says, "what if it turns out that *that* is God's will too!" He clutches at his head in frustration. "How do I know what is really the wrong thing to do?"

Gloria swallows the last of her drink and presses the discreet button for Connie's return. She struggles to her feet, pulling her muumuu over her knees, and takes Lucifer's martini over to him where he now stands staring moodily out the window. "I know exactly what you must do," she says as she watches him drain his glass. "You must do exactly what I say."

Lucifer narrows his eyes with suspicion. "If I obey you instead of God, I might as well be bowing down to Adam!"

"Believe me, I am nothing like that hapless—Connie, no!" Gloria shouts as she and Lucifer turn back to face the room.

Connie, who has slipped back into the room unheard, stands beside the coffee table. Instead of removing Gloria's empty glass, she holds the small corked bottle in her hands.

"Connie, please, you don't know what you've got there!" Gloria says.

"Don't I?" Connie says. Her lips curl into a smile, something Gloria has never seen before adorn her housekeeper-of-twenty-years' face.

Gloria's own face turns white. She speaks very slowly.

"Connie, why don't you just put the bottle down on the table."

Connie slips the bottle into her apron pocket, sits down on the chaise lounge and kicks off her clunky orthopaedic shoes. "Why don't you just mix me a martini," she says.

Acts of God

From: Mrs. Alyssa Verbeek
To: Cosmic Insurance Ltd.
To Whom it May Concern,

I wish to make a claim for losses suffered as a result of a series of poltergeist attacks occurring at my home between June 21 and August 2, 2018.

On the evening of June 21, a rain of stones ranging in size from pea to golf ball fell on the house for a period of two hours, resulting in damage to the roof and a cracked skylight, which will cost $5,000 and $750 respectively to repair and replace.

In the early morning hours of July 2, various volumes of ectoplasm manifested in all the household drains; subsequent flooding in the basement and bathrooms located on the first and second floors incurred damage that will cost $10,000 to repair.

On July 11, I awoke to discover havoc had been wreaked in the kitchen. Graffiti was carved in the granite countertop with my best knife, which will cost $3000 and $250 respectively to replace. Also, amidst the general disarray, the salt and sugar had been switched; the wedding cake business which I run from my home suffered a loss of $300 for a product deemed unacceptable by an irate bride, as well as approximately $5000 in future business due to reputational damage.

In the afternoon of July 27, poltergeists invaded our sixty-inch plasma television, so that no matter which channel is on, it shows an episode of *Sesame Street* in Esperanto. The television will cost $2500 to replace.

The final attack occurred on August 1, when poltergeists took possession of my iPhone, sending texts, involving childish toilet humour, to all stored contacts, including current and potential business clients, and changing the ringtone to "Every Breath You Take" by The Police. The phone will cost $700 to replace. I estimate that an additional $5000 in future business prospects was lost as a result of the potty texts.

Sincerely,
Mrs. Alyssa Verbeek

From: Cosmic Insurance Ltd.
To: Mrs. Alyssa Verbeek
Dear Mrs. Verbeek,

I regret to inform you that your claim for losses incurred between June 21 and August 1, 2018 has been denied. I have reviewed the details and concluded that the sequence of events described constitutes an "Act of God" which is not covered by your current policy.

Thank you for choosing Cosmic Insurance.

Sincerely,
Orlando Blunt, Senior Claims Adjuster

From: Mrs. Alyssa Verbeek
To: Cosmic Insurance Ltd.
Dear Mr. Blunt,

Your suggestion that the series of malicious attacks against my household described in my claim were instigated by God is ludicrous. These acts, and their ongoing effects on myself and my family were distinctly malevolent in nature. Consider the following:

1. The sinister lyrics to that ringtone: "Every breath you take, every move you make, *I'll be watching you.*" (Italics mine)

2. My son, who attended Esperanto camp last summer, swears he heard Kermit the Frog say: "I am Legion,"

and that the episode of *Sesame Street* shown was being brought to us by the number 666.

3. Although the symbol carved in the granite countertop was a smiley face, the sharp angle of the eyes gave it what is universally recognized, even by infants, to be an expression of menace.

4. As a result of the ectoplasm manifestation, my daughter has developed a pathological fear of Jell-O for which she is currently being treated at a psychiatric institution.

5. My husband is no longer able to enjoy playing golf because the flying balls remind him of the frightening hail of stones.

There can be no doubt that the perpetrator of the attacks against our selves and property is Evil, and therefore not God. Attached please find an affidavit signed by Father Torvald Wilton verifying the Satanic origin of the poltergeists.

Sincerely,
Alyssa Verbeek

❧

From: Cosmic Insurance Ltd.
To: Mrs. Alyssa Verbeek
Dear Mrs. Verbeek,

In Isaiah 45:7, God says: "I form the light, and create darkness; I make peace, and create evil." Furthermore,

Biblical tradition claims that God created the angels, Satan among them. Therefore, even if the perpetrator of the events described in your claim is Satan, or another evil entity, ultimate responsibility for his / her actions clearly lies with God.

    Yours truly,
    Orlando Blunt

From: Mrs. Alyssa Verbeek
To: Cosmic Insurance Ltd.
Dear Mr. Blunt,

Your reading of scripture is regrettably literal and narrow-minded. The passage you quote is a translation from the original Hebrew which modern scholars have more accurately interpreted in a variety of ways which do not reference evil. According to Saint Augustine, "evil [is] nothing but a privation of good," meaning that evil is the *absence* of God.

    Sincerely,
    Alyssa Verbeek

From: Cosmic Insurance Ltd.
To: Mrs. Alyssa Verbeek
Dear Mrs. Verbeek,

Even if I were to concede that God did not create evil,
you have failed to provide conclusive evidence that all
the damages incurred on your property were the result
of poltergeist activity, and not caused by various other
means.

Best regards,
Orlando Blunt

From: Mrs. Alyssa Verbeek
To: Cosmic Insurance Ltd.
Dear Mr. Blunt,

Hello? Ectoplasm? What other possible cause do you
suggest? The earliest recorded poltergeist activity
occurred in ancient Egypt and involved stones raining
from a clear sky—exactly like those that damaged our
roof and skylight. Kitchen shenanigans have been
common poltergeist pranks throughout history; a much
publicized recent case in Coventry, England involved pots
and pans flying about and cupboard doors being pulled
from their hinges. If you've ever seen the movie *Poltergeist*
you'll know that televisions are a favourite medium for
delivering their sinister messages. Poltergeists are also

infamous for their ability to adapt immediately, employing new technologies, like smartphones, as fast as humans invent them.

Sincerely,
Alyssa Verbeek

From: Cosmic Insurance Ltd.
To: Mrs. Alyssa Verbeek
Dear Mrs. Verbeek,

Our own research department's investigation of the history of poltergeist phenomena reveals that prominent psychologists, beginning with Nandor Fodor in the 1930s, attribute the disturbances not to supernatural forces, but to human agents suffering from intense anger, hostility or latent sexual desire. Women and pubescent girls are most often to blame. It is possible, Mrs. Verbeek, that you yourself, albeit subconsciously, are the source of the reported activities, in which case your claim for losses incurred would be considered not just invalid, but quite possibly fraudulent.

Sincerely,
Orlando Blunt

From: Mrs. Alyssa Verbeek
To: Cosmic Insurance Ltd.
Mr. Blunt,

I deeply resent your suggestion that I am a) dishonest, and b) sexually repressed!

To disprove the former allegation, I would be willing to subject myself to a polygraph test, but I fear the temptation for the poltergeists to interfere in such an event would be too great, hence the results would most certainly be skewed. As to the latter, I will be happy to meet with you personally to provide evidence that will surely persuade you that your accusation is untrue, as long as my husband does not find out, since I do not wish to add to the trauma he has already suffered.

    Sincerely,
    Alyssa

From: Cosmic Insurance Ltd.
To: Mrs. Alyssa Verbeek
Dear Mrs. Verbeek,

Cosmic Company Policy forbids personal contact with clients in such cases, to prevent transmission of evil spirits.

A secondary panel has now reviewed all details and documents of your case. I regret to inform you that the original decision to deny your claim for losses has been upheld. This decision is now final.

Thank you for choosing Cosmic.

Sincerely,
Orlando Blunt, Senior Claims Adjuster

⚜

From: Mrs. Alyssa Verbeek
To: Cosmic Insurance Ltd.
Dear Mr. Blunt,

Your decision is indeed regrettable, as I'm sure you realize with improved clarity this morning. I do hope your wife wasn't too frightened by the pounding on your roof and windows last night. How does she feel about slime?

Cheers,
Alyssa Verbeek

Life of a Saint

"If you had a spiritual practice of your own, you wouldn't be so dismissive," Jenna snarled. "It would give you the gratitude and humility to understand, and maybe your life wouldn't be such a disaster!"

Georgina knew she shouldn't have come to her sister's Hallowe'en party. She could feel the other guests agreeing with Jenna's assessment; they might as well have shouted "Hear! Hear!" Georgina was the only one in the room who did not own a house, or a car, or a stock portfolio; she had no husband, no children, not even a dog; there were no letters behind her name and her CV was a disgrace. Yet she'd had a promising youth. Before she was kicked out of university because the dorm manager discovered the marijuana Georgina's boyfriend had stashed, unbeknownst to her, under her bed, she'd been maintaining straight A's.

She decided at the time to take advantage of the situation and concentrate on building a career as a performer, which had always been her real dream. She tried every kind of performance imaginable, from community theatre, to stand-up comedy, to recording a desultory hip-hop album in a friend's basement, but the dream just never panned out. At age thirty, she gave school another try, enrolling in a glass-blowing course at a community college. The third time she singed off her bangs, eyebrows and eye lashes, she dropped out. Her most recent failure involved a YouTube cooking show.

Her history of relationships was an even bigger catastrophe. The campus pot dealer was followed by a bigamist, bisexual banjo-player who, unbeknownst to Georgina, had a wife and child in Vancouver, and a husband and child in St. John's. Then there was the magician who made her savings account disappear, and the stockbroker who broke her nose.

Her longest relationship was with Brian; it lasted nearly seven years. Though Georgina considered that period the happiest of her life, to her family and friends, it was her most notorious indiscretion. Brian was twenty-six years her senior; worse, he was married to Jenna's husband Craig's aunt Tilda. Their affair commenced in the cloakroom at Craig and Jenna's wedding, the mother of the groom discovering the couple in passionate embrace, Brian's hand under the raised skirt of Georgina's avocado bridesmaid dress.

Jenna's spiritual practice was of a strictly non-religious kind: yoga, recycling, and local organic food. (Georgina had violated her BYOLB—Bring-Your-Own-Local-Booze —proviso for the party by turning up with a bottle of Russian vodka instead. No way was she going to spend Hallowe'en sipping artisanal beer or chewy homemade wine.)

Most recently, that spiritual practice had involved

forming a positive energy circle around Jenna and Craig's son Oliver's hospital bed. Oliver had been attending Kalaripayattu martial arts and dance camp when he collapsed, two months ago, and was rushed to hospital to undergo emergency surgery for a burst appendix. The septic shock that followed nearly killed him. Craig and Jenna issued a Facebook request for volunteers, and although she was sceptical, Georgina put in four three-hour shifts, holding hands with various other members of the couple's support group, humming and chanting and focusing healing energy on the sick boy.

Since their births, Georgina had been bombarded with Jenna's boasts about her perfect children Oliver and Sophia. Their moulding had begun at the moment of conception through a series of educational CDs, from *Enlightenment for Embryos* to *Team Building for Toddlers*. Now eight and five, they were both star pupils at their elite French immersion Montessori school. Oliver was also fluent in Mandarin and very accomplished on an Andean stringed instrument called a Charango, while his sister displayed prodigious talent in mixed media collage. They kept rigorous schedules of stimulating activities to optimize the formation of neural connections in their still plastic young brains, they wore only natural-fibre clothing and ate strictly organic foods. As Jenna said: "No pesticide or GMO has ever passed their lips." Which is why she snapped at her sister when Georgina observed that the antibiotics probably had more to do with Oliver's recovery than their chanting *Om Namaha Shivaya*.

Nervous about facing Craig and Jenna's smug friends, Georgina had already downed three crantinis in quick succession, which put her at a disadvantage now that her sister had publicly called her out. It wasn't true, she thought. She did indeed have a spiritual practice: failure. She was practically its patron saint! Nothing taught one humility more thoroughly than that. She lifted her glass. "To my disastrous life!" she said, then missed the rim of her glass with her lips as she attempted to take a sip, spilling vodka and cranberry juice down the front of her sexy devil outfit. It had seemed like a great idea in the costume shop, less so now that she stood next to Jenna who was splendidly attired as a functional wind turbine.

Jenna kissed her teeth with disgust and went to find a cloth. Georgina picked up her tail and slipped red-faced from the room, overhearing Jenna's friend Barb say: "You'd think the devil would know a trick or two for getting rid of cellulite."

She crept away from the party to a dim back hallway and found the door to the sun porch. Inside she leaned her back against the wall and breathed deeply; she knew it would be cooler in there. The weather was exceptionally warm and humid for Hallowe'en; the heat in the house packed with noisy revellers had become unbearable. Dizzy and disgraced, she just needed a few minutes to re-gather her wits. She closed her eyes and fanned her face with her hand.

She missed Brian. Everyone knew Brian's wife Tilda was a tyrant, so no one blamed him for seeking something more. But they didn't hesitate to blame Georgina, especially when Brian left his successful law practice to follow his dream of running a hot air balloon company. They were still blaming her when Blow Hard Balloons went bankrupt within the year. At least they couldn't hold her responsible for the leukemia that eventually took his life. There was no positive energy circle for Brian when he lay dying in a cancer hospice, though Craig and Jenna did bring Oliver and Sophia through for a perfunctory goodbye. Only Georgina stayed with him until the end, stroking his hand and humming "Up, Up and Away" as he passed on. Then she was alone again, and devastated.

Suddenly, she had a creepy feeling that she was not alone. Her eyes flew open. There were no lights on in the sunroom, but the moonlight through the windows was so bright she didn't need artificial light to see him clearly, her nephew Oliver. He'd always been scrawny for his age and he'd lost weight during his recent time in hospital. He wore a tight hood over his head that looked like a striped sock with a circle cut open for his face. There was a large mound of Hallowe'en candy on the table in front of him and wrappers of candy already consumed were scattered all around. He looked up at Georgina with big, uncanny eyes and popped a fun size Mars bar in his mouth.

"Oliver! What are you doing up?" Jenna was always bragging that her children were in bed and asleep before eight-thirty without fail.

"The noise level is not exactly conducive to sleeping," Oliver said between chews.

"No, I guess not." Georgina reached forward unsteadily to grab hold of the back of the chair opposite him. "Do you mind if I sit?"

"Be my guest."

She lowered herself cautiously into the chair, sighing heavily, then removed the false eyelashes — the real ones had never grown in properly — that were irritating her eyes. As she grew accustomed to the dim, she perceived an odd circle of padding at Oliver's back that pushed him forward toward the table. "What are you supposed to be?" she asked.

He rolled his eyes. "A midland painted turtle. Part of the one-of-a-kind indigenous Canadian wildlife collection designed by my mom's friend Barb. Sophie was a red breasted nuthatch."

"A nuthatch. That's a bird, isn't it?"

"Try telling dopey Sophie that. She was convinced — because of the 'nut' — that she was supposed to be some kind of squirrel, the beak protruding from her forehead notwithstanding."

"I'm guessing it wasn't your first choice, being a turtle."

"I wanted to be a zombie. But Mom said that wasn't very *affirming*."

"At least you got to go trick-or-treating," she said, gesturing to the pile of candy. "I thought you weren't allowed to have junk food."

"We had to go while it was still light. Nobody else was out yet. We had to keep waiting for people to get their candy out of their cupboards and rip open the bags." Oliver rolled his eyes again. "It was so embarrassing."

Georgina smiled. "Well, you can hardly blame them for being over-protective. You almost died in the summer."

"Actually, I did die," Oliver said. "I was dead for a while, but then I came back."

"How do you know you were dead?"

"I floated up above my body and could see everything that was going on." Oliver ripped open another fun size chocolate bar, Coffee Crisp this time, and popped the whole thing into his mouth.

"Maybe you were just dreaming," Georgina said.

Even in the moonlight she could perceive the look of resigned patience, as one might use with an uncomprehending child, on Oliver's face. "I saw and heard things that I couldn't have known if I was asleep. For example, I saw you, with your crazy shoes."

Georgina's pencilled-in eyebrows flew up. She'd arrived for the positive energy circle dressed, typically for her on a hot summer day, in a pale yellow sundress and a pair of orange and yellow platform sandals. They were, admittedly, a bit crazy. Jenna had looked at her shoes and said: "Are those really appropriate?" Georgina would have thought bright colours most appropriate for a positive energy circle, had she thought about it at all, but everyone else was dressed in dark sweats or leggings and flat practical shoes, as if they were ready for a workout.

"What colour were my pants?" Georgina asked, figuring Jenna might have told Oliver about the shoes.

"You were wearing a dress and it was yellow," Oliver said. "And you snuck into a laundry closet and drank from a flask between sessions."

That was something she was sure Jenna didn't know. "So what else happened? Did you just float around the hospital?"

"I went up. I could see more and more the higher I got."

"So did you go to heaven?"

That resigned but patient look again. "I had a meeting with my spiritual advisors. They arranged the whole thing — the appendectomy, the infection, etc. — because they needed to talk to me. It seems I was getting a little off track in life."

"You? Off track? That's hard to believe."

"One's intended path in life is not as obvious as people

generally think," Oliver explained. "Often it's the ones you least expect who are actually getting it right." He ripped open a miniature bag of potato chips and poured them into his mouth, as if he were drinking them, scattering crumbs every which way.

"Who were these spiritual advisors?"

"It was a panel of experts on various life issues. You only know two of them."

"I do?" Georgina said, surprised. The music from the party stopped for a few moments before starting up again with yet another reedy-voiced alt-rock singer-songwriter no one could possibly dance to.

He nodded as he tossed the chip bag over his shoulder and reached for a peanut butter cup. "Great Uncle Brian," he said.

Georgina was too flabbergasted at first to reply. Was this a precocious joke he was playing on her, she wondered. But she didn't think he was aware of her relationship with Brian. He was only six when Brian died. And he looked perfectly serious. "And Darnley," he added.

"Darnley? Darnley the difficult dog? But—"

"Mom thinks I don't know he's dead."

Craig and Jenna had conducted a voluminous amount of research and visited eight different breeders before choosing a golden labradoodle puppy custom designed to suit their "values and lifestyle." Labradoodles, Jenna explained, were highly intelligent, easy to train and hypo-allergenic. Darnley proved to be anything but. His fur gave Sophia the sniffles, he flunked obedience school three times, he peed on anything or anyone new brought into the house—not out of rancour, but as a gleeful sort of greeting—and he ate everything in sight. When he started dinging every time he moved, Jenna and Craig deduced the whereabouts of a missing decorative copper bell, and took him to the vet. The subsequent surgery uncovered, as well as the bell, a sippy-cup, a pair of Elmo slippers, and Craig's grandmother's antique engagement ring.

Georgina harboured secret delight at Darnley's ebullient refusal to bend to Jenna's will, but was appalled when they eventually had the dog put down. They told Oliver and Sophia he was going to live on a farm where he could pee wherever he wanted.

"What did Brian and Darnley advise you to do?" she asked.

"The particulars are quite personal," Oliver said. "Suffice it to say I learned to change my ways." He ripped open a package of red licorice and chewed through it rapidly.

"Are you supposed to be eating all that?"

"Nope. We're only allowed to have one treat every three days. It'll probably keep me up all night."

Georgina laughed, then Oliver laughed too, which made her laugh even more. She laughed until there were tears running down her face.

"Hey," he said when they finally calmed down. "Can I try your horns?"

She touched her red sequinned devil horns. The plastic hairband on which they were mounted was digging into her skull behind her ears. "You can keep them," she said, removing it. She reached over, pushed the turtle hood off Oliver's head. His fine, angelic blonde tresses stood up every which way with static electricity. She slid the horns on and he grinned again, a perfect little devil.

"Thanks," he said. "Here, help yourself." He pushed an assortment of candy her way.

"That's very generous of you," she said, choosing a mini Caramilk.

"Not really," he said. "This is Sophie's stash."

Acceptance

It is such an honour to be singled out for this award, especially after so many years of closed doors and rejection after rejection. So first of all, I'd like to thank you all for that rejection. Without it, I might have won this award years ago and slacked-off, living off the spoils, instead of struggling to pay the rent, scrabbling for even a can of chickpeas for dinner.

I'd also like to thank my parents, Dick and Linda Woodward sitting right there in the front row, for always favouring my sister Emily. I learned from a very young age that I would never be loved for myself alone. I don't blame you. I was high-strung, and felt things deeper than most, like when our hamster Hampstead died. Emily was content to skip off to the pet store to find a replacement, but I was inconsolable. I could tell by looking into his eyes that the new Hampstead was an imposter—I wasn't as gullible as sunny, obedient Emily. It was only natural that you would love her more. It made me realize that I would have to do something remarkable to win your attention, so thank you Mom and Dad.

Thank you also to Mr. Ruddick, who was our next-door neighbour when I was a child. We never really had a conversation apart from when he would yell at me to get out of his vegetable garden. But when he died, and we went to visit him in the funeral home, his was the first dead body I had ever seen. When no one else was looking, I slipped a letter to God into his pocket as he lay in the coffin, a letter in which I asked for precisely this honour, that I would one day win this award.

Now I know that he did indeed deliver my petition to heaven by hand. Don't get me wrong, folks, I do believe in the regular kneeling-by-the-bed-at-night method of prayer, but I imagine an awful lot of you here have prayed for the exact same thing—not least my fellow nominees—yet I'm the only one who's actually up here now, aren't I? Obviously this request required special measures. So thank you, Mr. Ruddick. And I'm sorry for trampling your Swiss chard.

A special thanks as well goes out to another person I haven't seen in over thirty years: Jennifer Woodley. I don't even know if that's her name anymore. She likely got married at nineteen, pregnant at twenty, trapped in mediocrity for the rest of her life—isn't that what happens to the cool girls who are at the top of the pecking order in Grade Six? It was the alphabetic proximity of our names that forced us to sit side-by-side the entire school year.

Every day of that year she ignored me until lunchtime. She'd wait for me to take a sip from my thermos before tickling me so that everyone could watch cherry Kool-Aid come out my nose. But as the bible says, the meek shall inherit the earth. My therapist, too, contends that humiliation is almost always a necessary precursor to greatness, so I thank you, Jennifer, for contributing this essential ingredient to my success. I'll be happy to do the same for you, if you'll just get in touch with my agent.

Thank you also to my gym teacher, Mr. Planters, for failing me repeatedly and laughing when I ran into the tetherball pole. Were it not for his disparagement, I might have been distracted by lesser pursuits, sports and childish games, instead of devoting myself fully to the life of mind and spirit. What he doesn't know, is that the mild concussion I suffered when I hit that pole opened up a door of perception and capacity for greatness that remains closed to most. Who's laughing now, eh Mr. Planters?

I would like to thank Amelia Earhart, whom I discovered through hypnotic regression I was in a previous life. By thanking her, it may sound to some like I'm thanking myself, but in fact, while we are the same eternal soul, each incarnation possesses a distinct personality with specific talents and needs. In recalling my experience as Amelia, I am able to access wisdom and information I am not otherwise aware that I have. Her—that is my—courage and enterprising spirit have inspired me in this incarnation. Without it, I would not be standing before you tonight. And yes, before you ask, that means I do know exactly what happened to her in the end, but I will not spoil the mystery for you, as that too is part of our legacy.

I'd also like to thank my ex-husband, Rick, for cheating on me, with one of my fellow nominees here tonight, no less. Familiarity with the full spectrum of human emotion, including betrayal, is key to doing the work that I do well, so thank you. And since I know thoughtfulness isn't your strong point, Rick, let me give you some advice: be sure to

remind your date that it's an honour just to have been nom-
inated.

Thank you also to the hitchhiker, purportedly named
Ron, whom I picked up on the Trans-Canada Highway halfway between Kenora and Thunder Bay. He may think he
pulled a fast one when he stole my car during an emergency
bathroom break, leaving me stranded miles from any human
habitation. But in fact, he was just a pawn in the universe's
grand scheme, the plan that would lead me to my destiny.
When I did finally get a ride home that night, it was not by
earthly means. It wasn't approaching headlights that spotted
me, but a dazzling beam from overhead, one that transport-
ed me instantaneously to the round ship hovering above.

The time has not yet come when I may reveal all that
happened on the spacecraft that night, or on numerous
subsequent visits, but I would like to thank my extraterrestrial friends for confirming what I always knew deep down
to be true: that I have a special role to play in the future of
humanity, and winning this award is just the beginning. I
thank them for conducting the procedures, which have
fine-tuned the faculties and powers required to carry out my
destiny. The ones with that magic wand thingy were particularly inspiring.

And above all this evening, I would like to thank God.
Some people think that the reality of extraterrestrial life
belies the existence of God, but the exact opposite is true.
The more common experiences of revelation described by
several of our traditional religions are simply microcosmic
versions of a macrocosmic glory that covers not just heaven
and earth, but countless other worlds. God has given me
this honour here tonight in part to provide a platform from

which I may share some of that with you. Now that you're finally listening.

So thank you all again for this truly humbling experience. I'll be happy to sign autographs for you all in the lobby.

Lucy's Head

After breakfast, Lucy's dad says, he is going to kill Lucy's hair himself. Yesterday, they walked to a place that burned Lucy's nose and the music was scraping and loud. A lady told Lucy to climb up onto a high chair then wrapped a plastic thing around her, a thing like a raincoat, except it was too tight around her neck. When the lady picked up her scissors, Lucy screamed until the lady told her dad they had to leave.

Lucy's raincoat isn't too tight; it's like a portable house that stands up around her, especially the hood with its beak that juts out over her face like a porch roof. She is like a snail, in her raincoat, carrying her house around with her wherever she goes. Her dad told her about snails and their houses and now she loves snails. When she wears her raincoat, she pretends she is a snail, wriggling back and forth inside to feel the protection of her shell until her mom tells her to stop squirming.

Sometimes the shell is too hot, like when they are inside

the streetcar. She wonders if snails ever get too hot in their shells. She can't stand being too hot. It makes her scream. If only she could make it cool inside her raincoat-shell. If she had a fan inside, like the one her dad puts beside her bed on very hot summer nights, then she could wear her shell everywhere, indoors and out. It would shield her from the people on the streetcar. She doesn't like it when both her mom and dad insist on holding her two hands, raising both arms up, like a bad guy, because then she doesn't have a hand free to cover her face if a streetcar person gets too close. Lucy tugs her hand away from her dad's, but her dad keeps grabbing it back and says Lucy, how many times do I have to tell you not to let go of my hand, and becomes exasperated. That means he lets out long, noisy gusts of air which sound like the word exasperated.

Her dad also becomes exasperated when Lucy doesn't finish her Puffed Wheat. She doesn't want Puffed Wheat, she wants Loot Froops. The pink ones are girls and the orange ones boys and they swim nicely in the bowl and in her mouth, but she's not allowed to have them anymore because once they are in her stomach they start to fight, and the pink ones climb up into her head like the girls she sees climbing to the top of the monkey bars that are like a horizontal ladder and sit there like a line of birds, dangling upside down by the knees. It aches when they are flipping around like gymnasts inside her head. It aches, but Lucy wants them anyway.

Her dad says she can watch television while he kills her hair, even though it's not television time. Lucy prefers the people in the television to the people on the streetcar. *On* the television, her mom and dad say, which is funny because she knows "on" means on top of. *On* the television is a green flower pot with a spider plant her mom told her not to eat because it's poison. But why would she eat a plant, especially one that is a spider? There are two different kinds of people in the television, the ones who can see her and the ones who can't. She can tell which ones can see her because they look out the television window and speak directly to her. The others just talk to other people in television and either they don't know Lucy is watching or they are pretending they don't know.

Like her dolls. Her dollhouse is very similar to the television, with walls on three sides and a roof on top, but open on the fourth side for her to see in. Unlike the people in television, Lucy can take her dolls outside the dollhouse, but it makes them very nervous and afraid. They prefer to stay inside and talk to each other as if Lucy is not there. She knows they are only pretending not to know she is there, because every once in a while one of them, usually the little girl with the long hair past her bum who is named Cassandra stands at the open edge of her second floor bedroom and sees Lucy's head, which is huge compared to the dolls' heads. Lucy's head is also bigger than the heads of the people in the television.

Lucy prefers it when the people in television talk to her. Her mom and dad always change the channel to cartoons or other kids' show, but the cartoons hurt her eyes, and the kids' shows always have puppets, which are disturbing. They have no bottom half. What Lucy likes to watch is called the news. She knows there is a relationship between what she sees on the news and where she lives. Lucy lives in Toronto. They sometimes talk about Toronto in television;

other times they talk about Africa and Iraq and China where she does not live.

Sometimes she sees fire in the news, and houses that turned to black sticks. She's glad her dollhouse is not in television, because she doesn't want it to turn to black sticks. Cars and buses get in television when they crash or get blown up by a bomber. Luckily, the dolls don't have a car and neither do Lucy and her parents. Her grandmas and grandpas have a big white car and a minivan, which is not mini because mini means small. Lucy imagines how sad it will be when one of their cars crashes or is bombed, and they are dead. Lucy knows what dead means. Killed. First you are killed, which is sharp; then you are dead, which is dull.

Once she saw very skinny mothers and children in television who had nothing to eat. Her dolls have nothing to eat. They have four plastic bowls and a frying pan and she can pretend they have food in there that fills them up so their stomachs don't hurt. But the skinny children can't pretend, so they cry. Some people in television shoot guns, boys especially. The boy doll doesn't have a gun though sometimes she imagines he has one hidden in his pocket and gets shot. Lucy is glad it is the boy doll who is dead and not Cassandra.

Lucy's dad puts the high stool from the kitchen in front of the television. She prefers to watch the news lying down on the couch on her belly so that she can squeeze her face in the crack where the back of the couch meets the seat cushion whenever commercials come on. The cool leather puffs against her ears and blocks the sound. Just like the earphones the doctor put on her head when her mom and dad were worried because Lucy wouldn't speak. The doctor gave her a bowl of marbles and said, every time you hear a beep, take a marble from the bowl and put it in the tray. The marbles were all solid coloured marbles, not like the ones she has at home which are mostly clear with little flakes of colour locked inside. Her dad calls those cats' eyes, so she won't touch them. She likes cats, but not when they have their eyes taken out.

When Lucy heard a red beep, she put a red marble into the tray. When she heard a yellow beep, she put a yellow marble into the tray. But when she heard a brown beep, she couldn't find a brown marble, even though she dumped the whole bowl in her lap to see, and the doctor became exasperated. Then Lucy had to look at a picture with rows of animals while the doctor put a cool black plastic spoon in front of one eye like he was going to scoop out her eyeball, so Lucy cried. Her eyeball would be cold and round like a scoop in an ice cream cone. Ice cream sometimes makes her eyeball hurt. Especially green mint ice cream. Her eyes are green, her mother always says, but Lucy knows they are also black and white. It must be the green part that hurts when she eats green ice cream. When the doctor shone a sharp light in her eyes, Lucy screamed.

The doctor had mean, buggy eyes; Lucy wished he would cover them up with black spoons. The doctor wanted her to walk on a board on the floor like a balance beam, but his buggy eyes made her fall off. She has seen girls in television, gymnasts on balance beams high up off the ground dancing and flipping. She likes those gymnasts, and figure skaters most of all. Cassandra has a dress like the girl figure skaters, though she doesn't have skates.

When her dad tries to lift her onto the high stool, Lucy

pretends she has no bones, so she is floppy like a sock. But her dad becomes exasperated and says, Lucy, if you don't cooperate and sit up you will lose your dollhouse privileges for a week. This means he will put her dollhouse in the hall closet where it is dark in the night and the day, and the dolls won't know when to wake up.

Her dad puts a towel around her shoulders and combs her hair. Then he chops some of her hairs with scissors, so they are killed, and Lucy screams. Lucy, he says, you don't have feeling in your hair. How does he know? She is the one inside her hairs, not him. She has more hairs than she has dolls or marbles or even Legos. Now all her hairs are going to be dead, so she cries.

Lucy, just watch the television, her dad says. Look, look what's on now. But all she sees in the television are puppets, their bottom halves chopped off just like her hair, so she screams.

Knowledge of Good and Evil
(proposal for a television miniseries)

After thirty years of sturdy but unremarkable service on the murder squad, Detective Inspector Edmund Puck's career takes a spectacular turn when he learns to communicate with his garden plants.

Handsome, in his early fifties, Puck lives alone in an old brick house in Toronto's Parkdale neighbourhood. It is the house in which he has cared for his elderly father for several years. He has no other family—his mother died when he was a young child—so when his father dies, the house and the back garden, which was his father's passion, become his alone. Women have frequently fallen for Puck over the years, but always find him emotionally unavailable, all the more so as he increasingly devotes what little time he gets away from his work to cultivating his father's legacy.

It is a shade garden, walled in by a two-metre-high fence, and anchored by a gigantic black walnut and a row of sheltering evergreens that keep the yard in perpetual twilight. A stone fountain in the shape of a large curled snake provides a soothing soundtrack of trickling water. In the heart of a rough neighbourhood, in a city plagued by increasingly violent crime, it is a haven, a little patch of paradise.

It is to this haven Puck retreats one evening in the middle of a difficult case involving a missing sixteen-year-old girl. A suspect has been arrested with the girl's bloodstains in his car. The police are sure he has killed her, but he refuses to tell them where the body is, knowing a murder conviction will be difficult without it. Puck sits by the fountain studying a photo of the girl in a prom dress, a large lily corsage on her wrist. "Where are you?" he murmurs out loud, then a flicker in his peripheral vision makes him look up suddenly. The light in the garden is fading, but he can still distinguish a tall pale lily, just like the one in the photograph. It's as if it is trying to tell him something.

The next day at the police station, Puck waits until his colleagues have left before slipping a polygraph machine into his briefcase. Back home in his garden, with the machine hooked up to his laptop, he carefully attaches electrodes to the lily's delicate leaves. He stares at the lily for several seconds before speaking.

"Can you help me?" he asks. He looks at the computer screen to see if the electrodes have registered a response, but there is nothing, so he takes out the photograph of the girl and places it carefully among the flower's petals.

"Do you know where she is?" he asks. There is a bleep as the computer registers a response. Puck unfolds a map of the city and places his index finger on a random point. Nothing. But as he moves his finger slowly across the page, the bleeps resume, weakly at first, and growing in intensity as he nears the target. He notes where his finger points when the response from the lily is strongest: a section of the port lands the police have not yet searched. The next day he leads a team to the site where the girl's body is located. The suspect goes down for life. Puck is hailed as a hero and promoted to Detective Superintendent.

The next case involves a young man brutally shot several times in the chest and stomach. There are numerous plausible suspects involved in a resurgence of gang warfare; the murder squad has been spreading itself dangerously thin chasing down so many leads at once. Puck hooks the polygraph to the lily again and asks whether it can identify the culprit. The lily does not respond. He tries showing it a graphic photo of the murder scene — still nothing. Looking around his garden, Puck notices how the crimson blossoms of the rhododendron mimic the pattern of bloodstains blooming on the chest of the dead man. He removes the electrodes from the lily and attaches them to the rhododendron instead, which quickly identifies the shooter among the suspects from their photos. The squad focuses its efforts on the individual and finds the evidence needed to clinch the case.

With each new case solved, D.S. Puck finds it increasingly difficult to explain his hunches, and toys with the idea of telling his squad the truth about his garden. He tests the waters with a colleague whom he spots misting the police station's single living plant, a scraggly spider plant. "Would you say that plant is achieving its full potential?" Puck asks.

"I'd say it's overreaching itself," he says, brutally snapping off a long tendril that's straying into a filing cabinet.

Puck concludes that neither his colleagues, nor the Canadian judicial system, are enlightened enough to admit the testimony of plants as evidence. So when the potted

Hindu rope plant he so carefully brings inside on the cooler nights tells him that the latest victim was strangled by her sister, Puck resorts to planting a strand of the sister's hair at the murder scene to convince his colleagues to investigate, and eventually prosecute her. Though soundly rebuked by the rope plant, Puck is never actually caught for this deception.

Nevertheless, suspicions surrounding Puck's uncanny success rate spread. When the boxwood hedge gives Puck the number for a bank account that links a corrupt mutual fund manager to the hit man he ordered to murder his accountant —she was locked in an airtight safe until she suffocated— Puck finds himself the object of a covert investigation. D.I. Rogan, who envies Puck's rapid rise through the ranks while his own career stagnates, convinces colleagues that Puck must be in cahoots with another trader implicated in the corruption scheme, taking some of the money that remains unaccounted for in exchange for ensuring the trader's immunity from prosecution. Puck is exonerated for lack of evidence, but resentment among his colleagues grows.

Rumours reach the local media when Puck heads up a high profile investigation into the murder of a political aide beaten to death with a large metal nutcracker. Suspicion quickly falls on the mayor and his wife who had been the aide's dinner guests mere hours before the estimated time of death. Their fingerprints, and those of the victim, were the only ones found on the murder weapon. Questioned separately, the couple explain how they inserted fresh walnuts into sliced figs and dribbled them with honey for dessert, as they lounged in the living room after dinner. The media publishes photographs of the mayor's wife with the aide at various political functions that suggest a close relationship.

Puck's colleagues jump to the conclusion that the two were having an affair, but Puck finds himself quite taken with the wife—whom he learns has something of a green thumb herself—and her teary denial of any inappropriate behaviour.

Puck's stolid defense of the woman's innocence is ridiculed by his team, so he turns, naturally, to his garden, and the wise old tree that is older than the house itself. But the ancient walnut is curmudgeonly and reticent about giving him any clear answers. Its branches are too high to reach with photos or other pieces of evidence. Puck invites the mayor's wife to see his garden, hoping that her presence will melt the old tree's heart. To Puck's relief, the tree tells him, after the woman is gone, that she is guilty of neither infidelity, nor murder. It was her husband who had the affair with the aide. But unbeknownst to Puck, the woman is photographed by a reporter as she leaves his house.

Although evidence of the affair between the mayor and the aide is eventually uncovered, and the mayor admits to killing him—without his wife's knowledge—for having threatened him with exposure, Puck's colleagues, and several media outlets, remain convinced that he could only have known of the affair from the wife, whom he must have seduced, and that he agreed to cover up her involvement in return.

Puck is forced into early retirement by his mutinying team; heartbroken, he must also give up all hope of friendship with the woman for fear of further impugning her character and inviting more media attention. He has nothing left but his garden, where he at least has the consolation of being reminded at every turn of another grisly crime solved.

Subsequent series may focus on a second career for Puck, as private eye or marriage counsellor.

Little Brother

Congratulations on your new Brain-Machine Interface (BMI) smartphone. By activating this technology you have already consented to our privacy policy.

We collect information from you every time you think, move, speak, connect, relate, emote, envy, wonder, covet, lust or dream. Our BMI-GPS records your physical whereabouts as well as all the sensory information you receive, and immediately calibrates the distance between your current situation and where you *wish* to be.

The information we collect from you may be used for any of the following reasons: to respond to your needs before you are even aware of having them, conveniently processing all charges to your credit card at the same time; to improve customer service, after all, we can always tell what you're really thinking; and to create an indelible record of your life so that you don't need to remember anything at all.

Occasionally, at our discretion, we will include third party products or services on our interface. WitFlix, for example, will deliver your favourite television shows and movies directly to your brain; you won't even have to open your eyes.

These third parties have separate and independent privacy policies, therefore we take no responsibility for their actions.

We do not sell, trade or otherwise transfer to outside parties your personally identifiable information. This does not include trusted third parties, like your therapist, for example, who finds the dreams recorded by our *Id* app most revealing. We may also release your information to government, military and law enforcement agencies, or any of the for-profit corporations contracted to do their jobs for them.

We will continue to collect information from you for the duration of your automatic lifetime contract. Penalties for early cancellation include fines, and repossession of all knowledge and experience acquired during our tenure. We are not liable for collateral damage to fine motor skills or happy childhood memories.

If you have questions or concerns, don't bother to contact us. We already know all about them, as do the appropriate authorities.

Changes to this privacy policy can be made at any time according to our whim.

Oracle

"**S**o the purpose of this meeting is to make sure we've got all the pieces and to clarify a few things before we determine your eligibility," Millicent said. She hated it when she caught herself beginning sentences with *so*—she had been an English major, after all. She slipped into the habit when she felt nervous. The woman facing her across her desk did not have a neck brace, a wheelchair or a white cane, like many of the applicants Millicent interviewed. Instead she looked as weary as a person could, with dark purple smudges beneath enormous, haunted eyes. Still, her short black hair was neatly combed, she was dressed simply but stylishly in black slacks and a blue blouse, and her shoulder bag was exactly the same as Millicent's own.

Katherine was her name, and though Millicent could see from her documentation that she was twenty years older than herself, she would have been hard-pressed to guess her age by her appearance. She could have been anywhere between thirty and sixty. Millicent wondered if she was called

Kathy, the way Katherines of that generation often were, unlike the Kates and Kateys among her own peers.

Millicent cleared her throat and began again, again ungrammatically. "Um, so you live alone, right?" She was unusually uncomfortable asking this question. She could see from the paperwork that Katherine was divorced, with no children; it felt like adding insult to injury to point out the woman's aloneness. Worse, Millicent realized too late that she was twisting her engagement ring around her finger. Would Katherine think she was flaunting it, throwing her own happiness in her face? She wasn't! Millicent had real compassion for these people. Not everyone had the privileges of education and support that she'd benefitted from. The waterfront view from the condo she and Dylan had moved into just two weeks ago flashed through her mind. Not everyone managed to make the right decisions in life.

"Your rent receipts look straightforward," Millicent said, looking studiously down at the file to hide her red face. "And all the financial information is here."

Katherine had been unusually thorough and diligent in preparing her application.

"Now about your income," Millicent said, raising her face again. "It says her that you were previously self-employed?"

"Yes," Katherine said. "I worked from home."

"And um, what was the nature of this work?"

"I'm an Oracle. I foretell the future."

Millicent had been trained to disguise her personal response to anything the clients said, but now her jaw fell open briefly before she became aware and closed it again. "Right. So you are unable to continue this work as an …

Oracle because of your current medical condition. Has your doctor filled out the forms—"

"It's all right here," Katherine said, removing a manila envelope from her bag and handing it across the desk. "Letters from both my family physician and psychiatrist confirming I suffer from PTSD."

"Post-traumatic stress disorder," Millicent said.

"That's the official diagnosis. Though in my case they should say *pre*-traumatic stress disorder, since some of the traumatic events I witnessed haven't actually happened yet."

This time, Millicent managed to keep her jaw closed. "Okay. So, the symptoms of your pre-traumatic—"

"Anxiety. Depression. Imagine how you would feel if you spent your whole working day, every day, seeing visions of catastrophe. All the pain, illness and shattered dreams doomed to befall every single client who came in your door. I come from a long line of Oracles. None of them had to go on disability, but we're getting a lot closer to the apocalypse now. Disasters right and left. There's only so much a person can take, even someone as spiritually advanced as myself. It's the flash-forwards that really get to me. They can come at anytime and are totally debilitating. I get the shakes and sweats, and I never sleep for more than two hours at a time without waking from a nasty premonitory dream."

Millicent had awoken early that morning from a troubling dream herself. She'd been standing in the tiny living room of the condo surveying the view, which was somewhat obstructed by her own reflection in the glass. Suddenly, the entire outer wall shifted outward, snapping apart from the building. It began falling, slowly and still intact, to the ground. To her horror, Millicent could still see herself in the pane of the glass as it fell, as if she was imprisoned inside its two dimensions, like the Kryptonian villains trapped in the mirror in *Superman*. She woke with a gasp before it hit the ground.

Dylan had reassured her just yesterday that the construction standards in their condo tower were superior to those in so many others around the city, which had seen a spate of shattered highrise windows already that summer, but Millicent found it difficult to shake the uneasiness of the dream.

"It's too bad, because I have a spectacular success rate," Katherine said. "You should see the testimonials I've collected over the years. Unfortunately, many of them had to be obtained from beyond the grave, from clients whose deaths I'd foretold. A shame, but at least they got what they paid for. My readings were accurate."

Millicent closed her mouth — it had been hanging open again — and cleared her throat. "The medical information seems to be in order. So, one of the things we can explore is whether there is other work you can still pursue, based on your skills, that would not be affected by your disability. What kind of educational background do you have?"

"I have an MA," Katherine said. "In English Literature."

Millicent disguised her sudden intake of breath by coughing into her fist.

"Not exactly a practical degree, I know," Katherine said. "But even if it were, the PTSD would preclude almost any kind of job, at this point. I have only to be in the same room as another person to start seeing scenes from his or her future. That's why I never need props, like tarot cards or crystal balls, that so-called psychics and fortune-tellers use. So many of them just tell clients what they want to hear. Not me. I only tell the truth, no matter how brutal." Katherine closed her eyes with a sudden wince, and began massaging her temples.

What did she see? Millicent noticed that Katherine was sweating profusely, her hands shaking. Dread rumbled in her stomach. Was it possible that Katherine was right now witnessing Millicent's future?

Millicent knew that terrible things—multiple sclerosis, opioid addictions, crates of nails falling from a forklift onto one's head—thwarted people's dreams and expectations every day. She saw these people, she helped them. But it had never occurred to her that she could become one of them. She had made good, realistic choices about her life. She'd supplemented her own Bachelor's degree in English with a diploma in Communications from a community college, instead of going to graduate school. And though she really preferred curling up with a good book, she always described herself as "a people person" in job interviews, to make herself more marketable.

Her current position was a one-year contract and there were rumours that she and several of her colleagues were to be replaced by kiosks once their contracts were up, but she had no intention of working for the government forever anyway. Dylan was working his way up in the financial services industry and would one day make far more than he did now. Millicent expected then to do work more in keeping with her interests. Some editing, perhaps. There was no need to worry about finding herself in a position like Katherine's. She had Dylan.

Of course, there were things about which she had

misgivings. Buying a condo they could barely afford in what many said was a real estate bubble about to burst had its risks. But Dylan was confident the market would continue to go up, and in his line of business, he should know. They'd taken out a devoted line of credit to cover the substantial cost of their wedding, which was in six weeks. She'd had her first dress-fitting on the weekend; she was a bit dismayed at the way it made her upper arms look fat, but everyone wore strapless these days. It practically wasn't a wedding gown if it wasn't strapless.

She hoped Dylan wouldn't notice—but of course he wouldn't. Dylan always flattered her on her appearance. Well, unless he was drunk and said things he didn't mean. Not that Dylan had a problem with alcohol. He was just young and carefree and liked to party. One of the reasons he was so adamant about the condo was that the entertainment district and all his favourite clubs were right on their doorstep. He could party on Thursday nights now, as well as the weekends, and still squeeze in a few hours of sleep before work on Thank-God-it's-Fridays. Millicent usually stayed home with a book. Which was fine.

As long as he didn't get too drunk at the wedding. As long as he didn't say anything about her arms.

If only she could ask Katherine about her future! That would be not just unethical, but cruel, like asking the man whose back was crushed by a crate of nails to help her move the furniture. But if Katherine could already see what was going to happen, it could hardly add to her trauma by asking for a quick summary. The damage was already done. Maybe Millicent could do a deal and promise Katherine's application would be approved in exchange. It occurred to

Millicent that Katherine must have foreseen approval of her disability support application; otherwise why would she go through all this trouble? It must be like living backwards, she thought, knowing exactly what was to come.

Millicent suddenly felt dizzy; the room seemed to be spin around her. "Excuse me," she whispered, as she stood and stumbled over to the windowsill where she kept a thermal pitcher of water filled at the cooler first thing each morning. She turned her back to Katherine and poured herself a paper cup full. Her hand shook as she raised it to her mouth. She didn't need Katherine's advice; she could see her own future stretching out ahead as plain as day — unemployment, money woes, and Dylan's mean drunken comments as her arms got fatter and fatter. Was it too late?

"Katherine," she said, her voice hoarse, as she returned to her seat. The Oracle reopened her eyes. "Is it ever possible to change the future?"

Katherine cocked her head and raised one eyebrow. They stared at each other in silence for a few moments before a knock at the door made Millicent jump again from her seat. The door opened and Millicent's boss Sandra entered followed by two uniformed police officers, a man and a woman.

"Millicent," Sandra said, in a strange hushed voice, "Beatrice is going to take over this file." Her colleague Beatrice gathered Katherine's application from Millicent's desk and asked Katherine to go with her.

Millicent's heart pounded as Sandra closed the door. How could she have heard? Millicent knew her question to Katherine was inappropriate, but it was hardly a police matter, was it?

"Please sit down," the female officer said gently. "Can I just confirm that you are Millicent Gillespie?"

Millicent nodded and gulped.

"I'm afraid there's been an accident," the male officer said. "Another windowpane fell from a condo tower on Bay. Dylan Rufus, your fiancé, I understand, was having a cigarette directly below. I'm so sorry, Ms. Gillespie."

Free Will

—9-1-1, what's your emergency?

—I killed my parents-in-law.

—You killed someone?

—Both of them, yes.

—Are you at 119 Victoria Street?

—Yes, that's it. It's their house. Jack and Donna Kochansky.

—Are you sure they're both dead? Is either of them breathing?

—Definitely dead. But I didn't mean to do it. I was asleep. I didn't know what I was doing. I just woke up a minute ago. When I realized what had happened, I called you first thing. I figured that was the right thing to do. Is someone coming?

—Police and ambulance are on their way. What is your name?

—Jessica. Jessica Brown. What's yours?

—It's Alan. You'd better stay on the line, Jessica. Is there anyone else in the house?

—No, just me and the bodies. My husband Dalton was here earlier, of course, for Christmas dinner. We always have Christmas dinner with his parents. Dalton insists. Because he's an only child, he says, they get priority over mine. I suppose he's right, though it means I miss my own family's Christmas, with my sisters and their kids. Have to settle for a visit on Christmas Eve. But it's not like I resent it, or anything. I would hate to think of Jack and Donna having their Christmas dinner by themselves.

They're good people, really. They brought up Dalton to be who he is, so they must be, right? You know, they still use Christmas ornaments he made in kindergarten to decorate their tree. They have all these little traditions that have to be exactly the same every year. God help you if you suggest the tiniest change, anything resembling progress! Ha-ha. It's true, though. The first Christmas after Dalton and I were married, I wanted to contribute something to the meal, so I found this lovely recipe for a pineapple flan that's extra fluffy and light, perfect after a heavy meal. But when we'd cleared away the dinner plates, Donna comes into the room with this towering meringue concoction that she's apparently been making for fifty years. Just left my dessert sitting on the kitchen counter, didn't even mention it. Instead, she serves out gigantic pieces of this heavy, sickly-sweet cake without asking if we even want it.

She considers it an insult if you don't eat the whole thing, and let me tell you, that's a challenge after turkey with two kinds of stuffing—sausage and oatmeal—potatoes whipped with gobs of butter and cream, glazed carrots, Brussels sprouts with maple sauce, mashed turnips, and—would you believe it?—*cabbage rolls*. It's a Ukrainian thing. Must have cabbage rolls with every meal. I'm not a picky eater, but if there's one food I hate, it's cabbage rolls. And the thing is, another tradition of the Kochansky household is that you're never allowed to serve yourself. No. Jack holds up each plate while Donna fills it, so everyone gets their proper share of everything, whether they want it or not. Every year I say, diplomatically of course, that I'll hold off on the cabbage rolls in case I don't have room; every year she plunks one down on my plate anyway. This year, she gave me two! Unbelievable! I wonder …

—Jessica? Are you still there?

—I was just thinking that those cabbage rolls are likely to blame for this situation tonight. They've upset my stomach. That's one of the theories, you know. The same way some foods can cause nightmares, they may also trigger particularly dramatic episodes of somnambulism. Dr. Paxton has asked me to take note of what I ate the night before whenever I become aware of sleepwalking. She's a sleep specialist, Dr. Paxton.

You could say I'm her star patient. My history of sleepwalking is, in her words, unprecedented. I've been a sleepwalker my entire life. In fact, my mother says I sleep-crawled before I could even walk. You wouldn't believe the things I've done in my sleep. Cooked myself grilled cheese sandwiches, walked to the corner store, painted the bathroom. I once drove all the way to Kingston—four hours on the road—woke up in the car parked in front of an old boyfriend's house. *Parallel* parked. Totally asleep the whole time. No awareness of what I was doing or memory of it when I woke up. Just like tonight. I have no idea how I got here. Last thing I remember is climbing into my bed at home.

—Where do you live?

—Just a few blocks away from here. Eight Gardiner Street. Ha-ha, isn't that funny …

—Jessica?

—Just peeking out the front window here, and there it is, my bicycle. Well, it's been so mild this December, it makes sense. It's only five blocks. And look at that, I even locked it to the fence out front. Isn't that funny! Dr. Paxton will like that detail. She's written papers about me, you know, for medical journals, though she never uses my name. The closest she'll come is calling me Patient J. She says she can't use my name because of patient confidentiality. But I wouldn't mind. It would be my fifteen minutes of fame. A little harmless notoriety. It might actually give my career a boost.

I'm a painter—watercolours mostly. I'd like to do more work in oils, but the smell is too strong for our little apartment—the neighbours complain. Someday I hope to have a proper studio. Of course, my sleep disorder has nothing to do with my work, but the art marketplace is so difficult, anything that draws people's attention is good. The sleepwalking might spark their curiosity, but once they took a look at my paintings, I'm sure they would consider them on their own merits.

So for now I work in a grocery store, temporarily, of course, just until I can break through, sell some work. Dalton works in IT. It's a pretty good job, enough to pay the bills, but we're trying to save a down payment for a house. We'd probably have enough to buy in some of the less expensive neighbourhoods in the city, but Dalton has his heart set on this area, close to his parents, so we'll be saving for a while yet. That's why we decided not to buy any Christmas presents for each other this year.

We already abolished Christmas presents for everyone in my own family—except the children, of course—several years ago. I think my sisters just got annoyed with me for always giving them my own paintings. My oldest sister is a high school math teacher; the other is a doctor, an ear, nose and throat specialist, in fact. Neither has any appreciation for art. They'd rather get a Cuisinart or a selection of artisanal olive oils, which they can afford to buy themselves, so the whole policy is pretty sensible.

I thought we should apply it all round, but Dalton wouldn't have it. He always buys his parents gifts, expensive gifts. Thinks about it months in advance. This year it was a telescope for his father and this special wood-working drill with a zillion different bits, some as small as needles for his mother. Donna actually calls herself an artist, would you believe it? When all she makes are these fussy little crafts. Her latest thing is wooden doll furniture, but the furniture is strictly for display, not even for children to play with.

Dalton thinks it's important that they keep themselves busy with these hobbies, but they've got heaps of money to buy anything they want themselves. I don't see why we should have to finance it. Donna's got a whole room full of expensive tools and gadgets—I can see them from here. She turned the biggest room on this floor into her studio. Even installed larger windows so she'd have more light.

—Where exactly are you, Jessica, in what part of the house?

—The upstairs hall, by the phone. This is where I woke up.

—And where are they, the victims?

—In their bedrooms. Separate bedrooms. Personally, I don't see how you can call it a real marriage if you're sleeping in different rooms in your own house, though I guess as you get older and have health problems that might disturb each other's sleep it makes sense. People need their sleep. That's what they say, but you know, scientists have no idea why we actually have to sleep. There are different theories to do with things like rejuvenation of muscle tissue, growth cycles, boosting the immune system, but none of them really explain why we have to lose consciousness.

Why isn't it sufficient to just sit quietly and rest? Great white sharks don't sleep. They have to keep moving all the time so that water flows through their gills. Some scientists think their brains do sleep, one hemisphere at a time. So maybe I'm part shark. Ha-ha. Seriously, though, I've got my own theory. I think sleep is proof of Original Sin.

—*Original*—

—Sin, yes. I'm not really a religious person—spiritual, I would say, but not religious—though we did go to a United Church sometimes when we were kids. I remember thinking, when I saw a little baby being baptized, that the idea of that baby as sinful, bearing the guilt of Adam, was ludicrous. What's more innocent than a helpless newborn? But as I get older, it seems much more plausible. There *is* something innately wrong. How else could it be that good people, people with nothing but good intentions, do terrible, evil things? It's evident all through history, from the biggest scale, like wars and genocide, to banal everyday things, like cheating on your taxes. People contribute to evil even as they try to do good.

And when I talk about striving to do good, I don't just mean doing right instead of wrong. It's also a question of quality. I mean, when God created the world then sat back and announced that everything he made was *good*, I'm sure he didn't just mean that it wasn't sinful. He meant that it was beautiful, it was impressive. But for us humans, we can strive and slave our entire lives to create something beautiful, every desire and will and effort aimed at that cause, and end up with something merely mediocre, or just plain bad.

Mediocre might be okay for some. I mean, you can be a mediocre doctor or teacher, or a mediocre 9-1-1 dispatcher, for that matter — no offense, Alan — but it's true, as long as you do your job competently, you can make a decent living. Not so for a painter. For a painter, mediocrity is death. Hell. No matter how hard you try, no matter how strong you will it to be otherwise. Why is that? Alan? I would think, in your job, that you encounter more terrible things than most.

— We see all sorts.

— So you must agree that there is something innate, something not subject to our conscious will. Something unconscious, like our experience of sleep. Do you dream a lot, Alan?

—I'm an average dreamer.

—And wouldn't you say that your experience in your dreams, aside from being wacky and amorphous, occurs without your conscious will? I don't just mean the things happening around you, I mean you do things in your dreams that are against your own will. For example, have you ever dreamt that you went to work naked?

—I have.

—Exactly. We spend nearly one-third of our lives asleep. One-third of our lives in a state in which we have no free will at all. Absolutely no control. Now imagine how much worse it is for me. Instead of just playing out in my unconscious mind as I lie in bed, this disorder that I have, this handicap, means my body acts out my dreams, acts totally against my will, all while I'm asleep. That's why I'm here, at three o'clock in the morning, five blocks away from my bed—not naked, thank God—but in my pyjamas. How embarrassing is that? Not to mention cold, brrr.

I wonder if I wore a coat to ride over. If I did, I must have taken it off downstairs, though I should have known better, even asleep. Jack and Donna are always so conservative about the heat. They turn it right down at night to near freezing. Dalton and I had to sleep here a couple of nights before we moved into our apartment. It was so cold, I had to wear a toque to bed. Well, I suppose they just want to do the right thing, conserving energy, being environmentally friendly if not exactly good hosts. I'm going to miss them.

—Can you tell me how they were killed?

—You know, it's the funniest thing. It was that drill Dalton gave to his mother. She spent half the afternoon today attaching and detaching all the different heads and drill bits, explaining in minutest detail what each one is good for. She just gushed about the narrowest one. It's so delicate, she kept saying. Perfect for attaching tiny hinges with miniature screws. Turns out it's good for other things too. The neatest of holes, very delicate indeed, right through the side of a human skull. Hardly any mess. I mean, I woke up holding the drill, yet my hands, my pyjamas are perfectly clean. Not a spot of blood … I hear sirens.

—Best to stay right where you are.

—You are taping this, aren't you?

—All 9-1-1 calls are recorded.

—That's good, because I might need it to prove my innocence. Make sure you don't erase it, okay?

—I won't.

—They're here. Coming up the stairs. Oh, hi officer … Alan?

—Yes?

—He wants to talk to you.

Discomfort Food

Life is full of suffering. People are innately flawed. The pursuit of happiness is doomed to fail, and we would all be more content if we just acknowledged and accepted this. Such is the philosophy behind The Reformed Diner.

This unique establishment specializing in Dutch cuisine is the brainchild of Bram Boonstra. Boonstra immigrated to Canada from the Netherlands with his family as a child. His parents crossed the ocean on a converted troop carrier with fourteen children and a grand total of fifty dollars.

"They really knew how to live," Boonstra says. "Hard work, honesty and humility. And they practised what they preached in every part of their lives. Even in the kitchen."

The family learned to speak English quickly by banning Dutch from the dinner table until every child had acquired the new tongue. Their aim was to contribute everything they could to Canadian society.

After a forty-year career in municipal waste disposal,

beginning as a garbage collector and making his way up to operations manager, one would have thought Bram Boonstra had contributed more than his share. But rather than retire, he knew he had more to give, namely the valuable life lessons inherent in Dutch cooking.

"I travelled all over North America to speak at garbage conferences. Never once did I come across a single Dutch restaurant. There was obviously a need."

His years in garbage disposal gave him a first-hand view of the futility of chasing a perfect state of happiness. All that exercise equipment, the briefly popular electronics and fashions end up as landfill when they fail to give their possessors a sense of self-fulfillment. The amount of food waste was the most shocking.

"Food is fuel, not frill. It was time we showed it some respect."

Boonstra set out to create an eating establishment that would be a model of frugality and realism, with a small hint of pride in his heritage. With the Reformed Diner, he has succeeded in doing just that. The décor is sparse, with heavy wooden tables and chairs and blue gingham tablecloths. A scattering of prints, mostly of windmills, hangs on the walls along with a couple of framed embroidery samplers. There is no piped-in music to accompany the meal, just the clomping of wooden shoes on hardwood floors, since the waitstaff are charmingly attired in traditional Dutch costume.

There are no menus, as there are no selections to be made.

"I grew up eating whatever my mother put in front of me, and I thanked her for it."

Every evening before he goes to bed, he devises a three-course menu for the following day; when customers walk into the Reformed Diner, they must do so on faith that he has chosen well.

For a starter, I am served a thick pea soup known in Dutch as *Snert*. It is bland, but wholesome. "I don't believe in disguising the taste of real food by piling on heaps of hot spices," says Boonstra. "Besides, you know what that leads to."

My empty soup bowl is removed promptly and replaced by the main course: *rookwurst* with *stamppol* and beetroot. Stamppol, literally "mash pot," consists of potatoes mashed up with kale, giving it the appearance of chewed-up green goo. If you can resist the natural urge to catapult a forkful at your companion's face and taste it instead, you'll find it has a flavour that can only be described as virtuous. It's best to eat the stamppol quickly before the juice of the accompanying beetroot stains it with an unappetizing bloody hue. The beetroot itself is reminiscent of sweetened mud.

The rookwurst, or smoked sausage, is tough and requires some chewing. But as Boonstra attests, work is its own reward. He prides himself on the fact that I won't eat anything in his diner I might be tempted to describe as "melt-in-your-mouth." The strong smoky flavour of the tightly bound ground meat evokes, as I'm sure it was meant to, the reality of the human condition and fate. Slight essence of sulphur, bouquet of roasting flesh.

But life on earth is not without its consolations: A small serving of sauerkraut on the side promises to grease the wheels of digestion.

Then, of course, there is dessert, the saving grace at which the Dutch excel. On this count, the Reformed Diner does not disappoint: some well-aged Edam cheese with biscuits, and a plate of *oliebollen*. Oliebollen are deep-fried lumps of sweet, raisin-flecked dough rolled in icing sugar. In Holland, it is traditionally eaten at New Year's Eve, but Boonstra likes to serve it throughout the year.

"To remind us," he says, "that the end could come at any time."

Laws of Gravity

"John Calvin believed prelapsarian man possessed supernatural powers," Michaela said.

Isaac preferred working the trees with Michaela because the others dropped apples on his head and shouted "Isaac Newton!" every time he descended the ladder to empty his basket. Repetition apparently rendered the joke even funnier. He and Michaela were the only Canadian workers. The rest, hailing from Jamaica or Guyana or Mexico, were in the country on temporary permits; most had been returning to this fruit farm each summer for years. Despite the skyrocketing unemployment rate, Canadians, for the most part, refused to do work like this. By this, his third day on the job, Isaac could understand why. His back and shoulders ached so much he had to suppress a groan each time he reached for another apple.

"What kind of powers?"

"'Those which would have been sufficient for the

attainment of heavenly life and everlasting felicity,'" Michaela said, quoting.

Isaac's life used to be felicitous, he thought, until he became one of the millions of casualties of the great Plague, the virus that had simultaneously wiped out the operating systems of every mobile device manufactured by what had been, until that moment, the world's largest technology company. He hadn't worked directly for the company, but for an advertising firm whose sole client was the technology giant. "I'm afraid we failed to heed the first and greatest commandment," his boss said as he handed out lay-off slips. "Thou shalt have a diversity of clients before thee."

Isaac's employment insurance benefits had run out two months ago and he'd been forced to move into his parents' garage — that's how he referred to it when he was feeling sorry for himself, which was a good deal of the time. In fact, the bachelor apartment *above* his parents' garage, for which he'd exchanged a two-bedroom waterfront condo in Toronto, was cozy and comfortable with all the necessary amenities. It was a good sight better than the wooden barracks, with minimal bathroom and kitchen facilities, in which the temporary farm workers lived. Still, Isaac couldn't help feeling that the world had wounded him.

"Everlasting felicity," Isaac said. "What you mean is immortality."

"Immortality describes the natural state of humanity before the Fall," Michaela said. "But I'm talking about the abilities we possessed before they were corrupted by sin. Not only did sin distort our natural faculties of intelligence and judgement, it also virtually eliminated what we would today consider supernatural enhancements, like extrasensory perception and precognition, for example. What Calvin was really saying is that our distinction between supernatural and natural is false. God meant for us to have all these powers."

Isaac had already observed Michaela's uncanny ability to lean around her ladder and grab even the hardest-to-reach apples. She seemed to defy gravity; anyone else's ladder would have tipped. Despite her slight stature and tiny hands, she was by far the fastest picker, faster even than the six-foot-plus Jamaicans who'd been working here for more than ten years.

By noon, Michaela had filled three times as many baskets as Isaac, as was noted by the farm manager Henk. Henk drove the vehicle known to workers as the "jitney" through the orchard to take the workers back to the sorting barns for lunch. The jitney appeared to have been constructed from a station wagon with its top removed and replaced, behind the front seat, with a large board. Workers had to hop on and hold on, and hope not to get any slivers in their behinds, or else walk all the way back to the barn which cut a large chunk of rest time from their thirty-minute break.

At the barn, the workers retrieved their lunches from a row of cupboards; Isaac was embarrassed by his insulated cooler bag with "Cool!" emblazoned in silver on the side, but not embarrassed enough to stop using it. He was fastidious about keeping his food at a safe temperature, especially the cold cuts and mayonnaise. He was self-conscious too, about the size of his meal compared to the meagre tubs of beans and rice the others consumed, but the work made him absolutely voracious. He couldn't imagine getting through the afternoon on anything less than the foot-long submarine, homemade cookies, two pieces of fruit and large thermos of sweet iced-tea his mother had packed.

Michaela ate a very small cheese sandwich, then excused herself from the picnic table and went to sit on the grass under a tree a few metres away. There she was joined by Winston, one of the Jamaicans. Yesterday it had been Miguel, the day before it was Lance. They appeared to engage in deep conversation; a few times, Michaela took hold of Winston's outstretched hand. Isaac strained his ears to hear what they might be saying, but the others were too loud; they were passing around a basket of "thirds"—apples too scabby or deformed to be sold—trying to determine which one most closely resembled Isaac's face.

It was harder to remount his ladder after lunch with his belly so heavy and full. Isaac wanted nothing more than to lie down in the shade and take a nap. But Michaela scurried up her ladder just as quickly as she had first thing in the morning when the temperature was twelve degrees lower. Her lunchtime conversations were none of his business, but Winston had been strangely quiet on the jitney ride back, and Isaac couldn't help wondering if there was a connection. His curiosity finally got the better of him.

"What were you and Winston chatting about?" he asked.

"I was reading his palm," Michaela said.

"Did you see his future?"

"I told him to be extra careful. I'm worried he's going to have an accident of some kind. It would be a disaster for him if he couldn't continue to do this work. He'd likely be sent home. Unlike us, foreign workers aren't eligible for workers' comp."

Michaela hopped down her ladder, emptied her basket

into the larger bushel and was back in place in the time it took Isaac to twist one more apple from a branch.

"Do you want me to read your palm?" she asked.

Isaac shuddered, not at the thought that Michaela might foresee an accident like Winston's in his future, but the opposite, that she *wouldn't* see anything, other than a continuing career in apple-picking, no other prospects in sight, to unfelicitous everlasting.

"When you read the future in someone's palm," he asked, "is it already inevitable? Or is it possible to change that future based on what you learn?"

"I'm a compatibilist," Michaela said. "I accept the apparent contradiction between determinism and free will as just another example of the absurdity of the human condition."

"It is possible to change the future you foresee."

"In my experience, yes."

At that moment Isaac spotted the biggest apple he'd ever seen. It would fill up the space of three regular apples in his basket. And it was beautiful: glossy green, just beginning to turn red. Perfect ripeness for eating—crisp with a tangy balance of sour and sweet.

"So if Adam and Eve had precognitive powers, why didn't they foresee the consequences of the Fall?" he asked.

"Maybe they did. Maybe they foresaw the alternative as well."

Michaela was honing in on the gigantic apple; Isaac was determined to reach it before she did. He leaned out precariously from his ladder, but his fingertips just grazed its skin. Desperate, he took one last stab. When the ladder toppled and he plummeted heavily to the ground, he broke a few crucial bones, but the prized apple was still in his grasp.

Wits' End

an excerpt from
The Charming Villages of England

Lesser known among England's picturesque holiday destinations is Wits' End, located in the hilly seaside county of Notshire. The village is replete with delightful examples of tumbledown architecture. Visitors can find bed and breakfast accommodations in many of the local homes; they tend to be damp and draughty, as several of them lack roofs, but they make great backdrops for photographs. Wits' End also offers unique culinary delights. Visitors may lunch on a savoury meat pie—its precise combination of ingredients a closely held local secret—known fondly as Fox-in-a-Corner. Patrons of Grimmer's Pub may indulge in Enders Ale, a locally brewed beer, which recently won first prize, at an international brewery competition, for Highest Alcohol Content. And of course, Wits' End is renowned for its distinctive brand of cheese; affectionately referred to as "Witty Cheese," this soft sheep's milk treat is famously redolent of nettles and old socks.

One of the most popular tourist attractions in the

village is a decrepit fortress built by the Normans on a location previously used to garrison both ancient British and Roman troops. More importantly, it is the site at which the Cheesemonger's Revolt suffered its egregious end. This little known, but culturally significant rebellion was engendered by Wits' Enders; fired up with true faith and passion for their craft, they marched to Canterbury to demand that the words "and cheese" be added to the Lord's Prayer. "Give us this day our daily bread and cheese," the parishioners of Wits' End recite to this day to honour the sacrifice of their forebears. And sacrifice they did. Most were burned at the stake while taunting crowds tossed wedges of Witty into the flames to melt alongside their flesh. Those who escaped the stake were chased home to the fort at Wits' End where the King's men laid siege. As it happened, there was nothing in the fort's larder but cheese and the rebel rump eventually perished of scurvy. A handful of their fallen teeth are still on display in the foyer.

A field on the north side of the village is the site of one of England's distinctive circles of colossal standing stones that are older than the pyramids in Egypt. This ancient monument is popularly known as Sceptic's Henge because of a unique symbol carved into the northernmost stone that closely resembles a question mark. The purpose of England's other stone circles is unknown, but the residents of Wits' End believe theirs was the sacred gathering place of the planet's first agnostics. Adherents of the old faith continue to gather each year, on the day after Christmas, to express their doubts, in song and dance, and to exchange unwanted gifts.

The intellectually adventurous will be inspired by the

legacy of one of Notshire County's greatest inventors, Patterson George. Models of George's time travel machine, flying car and nuclear fusion reactor are on display in a museum dedicated to his genius. Of course, it is well known that, because of Patterson George's severe dyslexia, his measurements always got reversed. As a result, none of his inventions ever actually worked, but in theory, they are brilliant. The Dyslexia Association of Notshire County also maintains a branch on the premises which can be accessed through the back door.

Finally, lovers of literature from all corners of the earth flock to Wits' End to pay tribute to England's most beloved authoress Emmeline Wary. *Blustery Cliffs*, Wary's gothic story of passion and young love tragically cut short, is one of the quintessential novels of the Romantic period. The book, of course, was never actually published, but Emmeline Wary's descendants, who form the majority population of Wits' End, can attest to its brilliance, and are frequently overheard in Grimmer's Pub doing exactly that. Visitors to Wits' End can tour Emmeline's modest cottage, sit at the desk where she penned her masterpiece, and see the stub of the very last candle she burned. But her fans are most often drawn to the cliffs that were her inspiration and the site of her untimely death. While walking out on the heath to meet her handsome young lover Basil—who'd been banished from the cottage by her father who thought Basil a useless layabout, Emmeline was caught in a gale and swept over the edge. She clung to a ledge by her fingertips, waiting for Basil to arrive. When he finally appeared and peered down on her pale and lovely face, she had only enough strength to murmur her last exquisite words of love, before slipping away to her cruel fate. It is said that the stone still bears scratch marks from her finger nails, and each year several of her devotees fall to their own deaths as they scour the cliffs of Wits' End to find and touch her prints.

Denial

—**W**hat is your full name?

—Trevor Thomas Trenton. TTT. Why would I lie about that? *How* could I lie about that, I mean, you've seen all my documents, done a thorough background check?

—It's just a control question for the polygraph to compare with the other responses.

—I see. So now for the real interrogation. Fire away!

—Why do you want to work for CSIS?

—Because I'm a poet at heart. As you may have surmised from my CV, suitable careers for poets are few and far between, but as soon as I saw your ad, I knew this was the job for me. What is a spy but an extroverted poet? Poetry is the most perspicacious mode of inquiry into the secrets of the human heart. Spying is just the same thing writ large, probing the secret heart of humanity as a whole. I believe my experience as a poet, albeit an unpublished one as yet, uniquely qualifies me for the role of secret operative.

—Did you falsify any information on your application?

—Are you worried that my Russian isn't as proficient as I claim? I learned Russian because I wanted to read the Russian poets. Anna Akhmatova, Osip Mandelshtam, Marina Tsvetaeva. Ask me anything in Russian, I'll prove it.

—Just answer the question I asked *in English*.

—Oops, sorry. No, I didn't falsify anything. My French is excellent too. It's all about words, regardless of language. Words are my weapons. A well-aimed metaphor can pierce the strongest armour, and I'm very skilled in that respect. I have no doubt I'll pass the firearms training with flying colours.

—Have you ever been fired?

—Yes, when I worked for a business school. My job was to tabulate course evaluation scores. Mostly data entry, very monotonous. The only opportunity I had to use my poetic skills was in interpreting students' hand-written comments. Those business students are shockingly in-eloquent. I got to know several of the instructors; I understood exactly what the students meant to say about them. So I took the initiative to clarify and elab-orate as needed.

—That's why you were fired.

—Ridiculous, isn't it? For *exceeding* expectations. I'm sure CSIS will be more appreciative of my ability to take in-itiative, which is so important when working independ-ently in the field. The other time I was fired—

—You were fired more than once?

—Yes. I was also fired from my job as a tarot card reader. Reading tarot cards is a lot like both poetry and spying, really. It requires sharp intuition and the ability to make connections others may not perceive.

— Why were you fired?

— A client complained when I predicted her imminent death. But it was there in the cards, clear as day, at least to anyone willing to face the truth. I don't believe in shrinking from the harshness of reality, and at CSIS, I'm sure I'll face realities harsher than most.

— Did the client die?

— I never got her last name, so I can't confirm it empirically, but I'm certain she died soon after. It was her fate.

— You've had quite a wide variety of jobs.

— It's amazing, isn't it? Such good experience for working undercover.

— Have you committed any undetected crimes?

— Yes. I once pulled the fire alarm to clear the room at a poetry reading. The most atrocious poetry you can imagine — that was the real crime, subjecting an entire auditorium full of people to that crap. And the poet had already gone twenty minutes over. My action was perfectly justified, even if it was, technically, a crime.

— You were never caught?

— No. In fact, I was praised by the firefighters when they arrived for taking charge and directing people to the emergency exits. It was a very orderly evacuation, with no panicking, experience that will serve me well at CSIS, when dealing with bomb threats, for example.

— Have you ever stolen anything?

— Yes.

— What did you steal?

— *A star of burning tail.*

—A star …?

—*of burning tail.* It's Neruda, in English translation, of course. I stole it for one of my poems. I know, I should have italicized it or something to indicate that it wasn't mine, but I didn't. I just took it. I really wanted it to be mine. It was wrong, I know, and I'm very sorry about it. Wow, it feels really good to finally get that off my chest. I've never told anyone about that before.

—This isn't a confessional.

—Oh, I know. I'm not Catholic. I was raised Presbyterian. We were supposed to confess our sins directly to God, instead of to priests with supposedly special access. Everyone is equal. It's much more democratic that way. That's what we're fighting for, isn't it? Democracy—that's what CSIS is here to defend.

—Have you ever made pornographic videos or photos of yourself?

—Whoa! I wasn't expecting that one!

—It's important to determine whether there are any means by which you could be blackmailed.

—Well, I'm sure the machine is going to tell you that I'm lying now, because I can feel I'm blushing just at the question! Really, I'm sure there are no such photos of me out there, but wow, this is just like when you're a kid and they tell you God knows not just your actions, but all your thoughts too. Right away, you start thinking things you don't even want to think. This is just like that, isn't it? I can say what I want, confess or not, and you will still know the truth. Does it make you feel God-like?

—*I'm* asking the questions.

—I wouldn't be offended if you said yes. Emulating God is an admirable quality, if you ask me. It shows real ambition. I used to be uncomfortable with God's omniscience, God as the ultimate spy, until I realized that he is also a poet. He created the world and all of us by speaking. Words again. Words becoming flesh. Creation is one big metaphor. Sorry, what was the question again?

—This is the last one. Have you deliberately lied at any time in the course of this polygraph test?

—Yes. Spies need to be able to lie undetected, right?

Prodigal

The white van that pulls up to the curb doesn't look like the one the Kidney Foundation volunteers usually use. The bumper sticker reading Headed for Heaven is particularly strange. But the young woman in the passenger seat rolls down her window and calls my name. She is beautiful, with red curls and the kindest grey eyes.

"Are you my ride?" I ask.

The side door of the van opens suddenly. Two large men grab me by the arms, haul me inside and slam the door shut again. "Drive!" one of them shouts as the other pulls a pillowcase over my head. The pillowcase is unnecessary. I am always woozy and liable to black out after dialysis; this time, as the darkness clouds my vision and I slump into the seat, my last thought is: *I must be dying.*

But I can't believe in an afterlife anymore, so when I come to at the sound of the van door opening again, I know I'm still alive and not—all evidence to the contrary—in hell. I am clumsily lifted out and crammed into a wheelchair. Someone uses strips of soft cloth to tie my wrists to the armrests. I feel myself wheeled up a ramp, then in a door, across a room, and through another door. Still blinded by the pillowcase, I can't see where I am, but I don't need to. The smell is unmistakeable: must, wet wool and furniture polish. I am at church.

There is a low murmur of several voices in the room as the wheelchair is manoeuvred into position, then a moment's hush as the pillowcase is removed.

"Colin?" Grandma stands in front of me, bent over to peer into my face. "How are you feeling?" she asks.

"Thirsty," I croak.

"Yes," she says, holding out a large glass of water with a bendy straw. I drink deeply—dialysis always leaves me with a raging thirst—until I empty the whole glass. "Herbert said you would be thirsty."

Herbert Welch. I've seen him a few times at dialysis. I noticed that he had his own roster of volunteers who came to pick him up after his appointments instead of relying on the Kidney Foundation like me, but I never recognized any of them. Not, that is, until two weeks ago when it was Grandma's turn. I saw her coming before she saw me, but I was trapped, attached to the washing machine-sized contraption by two needles, one draining my blood, the other returning it to my body clean. When Grandma saw me—for the first time in over ten years—her eyes grew wide and she shrieked my name before falling to the floor in a dead faint, as though she had just been dialyzed instead of me. In the ensuing flurry of activity around her, I managed to stop the dialyzer, detach myself and leave unnoticed. I thought I'd had a narrow escape, but Grandma must have talked to someone at the clinic and obtained information about my schedule.

I went to live with Grandma after my parents died in a car accident when I was eight, though in truth we spent as much time at her church as at her house. I'd never been to church before that. I was alternately terrified and enthralled by the sonorous sermons of Pastor Don: afraid that my parents' death was punishment for my sin; fired with the hope that if I only prayed hard enough, my parents would return. When I was eighteen, I met Lucinda, who placed a circle of kisses all the way around my face and told me to stop tormenting myself.

"You did nothing to deserve that. If there was a God, your parents wouldn't have died," she said.

"Are these really necessary?" I ask Grandma, bending my hands up to indicate the wrist ties.

"Just until you've heard what it is we have to say," says a booming voice from behind my chair. I can't believe it: Pastor Don. He must be older than Grandma, and she's nearly eighty. He steps around the wheelchair so that he, along with Grandma and the entire congregation seated in the pews are facing me.

"Colin," Pastor Don says, "we want to give you a kidney."

"We?" I ask. "It's not like you can pass around the collection plate and each person contributes a bit. The whole organ has to come from one donor."

"We are aware of that," Pastor Don says. "And as individuals we may not be suitable donors, but collectively, there's a good chance we'll come up with a kidney that will be an excellent match. We are, after all, one body—the Body of Christ."

"You want to give me Christ's kidney?"

"Yes," Pastor Don says. "That's it exactly. Before being tested, we all signed a pledge that the one identified as the best match would provide the kidney. Your nephrologist has the test results and she assures us there is at least one suitable candidate among us."

"Dr. Armstrong is in on this?" I'm shocked. "She didn't say anything."

"She agreed not to get your hopes up before we knew we had a match," Grandma says.

"How did you find out who my nephrologist is?" I ask.

Grandma just smiles and shrugs. Herbert again. He is one of Dr. Armstrong's patients too. Dr. Armstrong asked me several times whether I had any family or friends who might be willing to donate. "I'll be blunt," she said. "There's a good chance you'll die waiting for a cadaveric kidney. A living donor is your best chance." But I told her there was no one, which was the truth. Grandma was my only relative; the cut-off age for donors is sixty, and she was long past that. So a cadaveric kidney was my only hope, and a slim one at that, given the supply shortage. It seemed inevitable that I would die soon and die alone and that would be the end.

Until now. I look out across the faces in the congregation. They all have the same expression of expectant wonder. The young woman with the grey eyes sits near the front; her face positively glows.

"What's the catch?" I ask.

"There's no catch. But there is something you must give in return. You must give Jesus your heart."

"Surely he can fix his own heart, being a miracle-worker. Why would he need mine?" I quipped, then felt ashamed seeing Grandma's disappointed face.

Pastor Don chuckles softly and paces in front of me with his hands clasped behind his back like I remember him doing while delivering a sermon. "Colin," he says. "I'm not going to insult you by telling you what you already know. If I remember correctly, you were a star Sunday school student."

"Indeed. I can still recite the books of the Bible faster than I can count to sixty-six. I know all the stories and how it's all supposed to work," I say. "The problem is, with all that's happened, I just can't believe it anymore."

"That's why we've brought you here today," Pastor Don says, lowering his voice, a professional trick that makes him sound more authoritative and his audience listen up. He picks up a chair that someone has put on the dais for this purpose, and sets it where he is facing both me and the congregation at the same time. When he sits down, they all shift forward in their pews. My heart pounds, but that may just be the usual aftermath of four hours of dialysis.

"You think you can turn me into a true believer with a life-saving kidney?" I ask.

"Think of it as positive reinforcement," Pastor Don says, "instead of threatening punishment with fire and brimstone. We're a modern church."

"But if I accept Christ as my saviour, how will you know I'm not just saying it to get the kidney?" I ask. "It's not like you can take the kidney back."

Pastor Don smiles. "God will know," he says.

Perhaps it is just my weakened state, but a shiver of fear runs up my spine at his words. I'm always exhausted after dialysis. It takes me the rest of the day and a good part of the next to recover — just in time for my next appointment.

"God can take the kidney back, if it is his will," Pastor Don says. "In fact, it happens all the time with transplants."

My eyebrows fly up. "Are you suggesting that when a body rejects an organ it is because of God's intervention?"

"God speaks in everything. If you're not a true believer, your body is sure to reject the body of Christ, just as sure as the devil cannot stand in His presence," he said.

I shiver again. Pastor Don doesn't look a day older than when I last saw him. There is still some black in his thick, silvery hair, and his face glows youthfully, without sags of drying skin. He still has a powerful effect on me, as surely as when I was a child.

"Colin," he says. "You're still a young man. What caused your kidneys to fail?"

I shrug. "It's nothing to be ashamed of. It was an auto-immune reaction that attacked and damaged my kidneys."

"Your body attacking itself," Pastor Don says. "Didn't that strike you as strange?"

"It's not common, but it's not unprecedented."

"It didn't occur to you that God might be sending you a message?" He looks me in the eye, as if he can see right inside me and I am trapped in that penetrating gaze.

The last time I saw Pastor Don before today was shortly after I moved out of Grandma's house and into a basement apartment with Lucinda. I never knew how he found me. "Living in sin," he said. Lucinda wasn't home, but her scattered clothes and collection of vintage handbags were clearly on display. "Do you know the wages of sin?" All I could do was nod dumbly and eventually he left.

Lucinda left too, when I became sick. She just couldn't live with the negativity, she said.

"But," I say, stuttering, "I can't just *decide* to believe, decide not to know what my rational mind knows."

"That's where you're wrong, Colin. We all have doubts. But you can ask for faith. You *can* decide to do that. And once you've joined the Body of Christ, once it is a living part of you, it is sure to make you a true believer."

"I thought kidneys made urine," I say weakly.

I look out again at the faces of the congregation. They all look so happy and hopeful. The woman with grey eyes rests her hands on the back of the pew in front of her. They are the most beautiful long-fingered hands. I imagine them stroking my face. Would it be so bad to go along with this? There was a time I would have stood firm, a time I thought hypocrisy worse than loneliness or death. Now in the stark face of both — and me not even thirty yet — Blaise Pascal seems very wise: Why not hedge my bets?

"Why do you want to do this?" I ask, raising my fingers in an attempt to gesture towards the congregation.

"I'm sure you know the parable of the prodigal son. It will give us great joy to welcome you back to the fold."

"But if I remember that parable correctly, there was a brother who wasn't entirely happy about the return. What if the person identified as a match is like that brother?"

"There are a few members of the church who could not find it within themselves to give. They were not tested and they aren't here today," Pastor Don explains. "Everyone here has agreed to donate. Ask them."

Several of them shout out: "We do! We want to give!"

The beautiful woman with the grey eyes shouts too.

Please God, I pray, *let it be her.*

Work-Life Balance

Memo to All Staff:

On behalf of the Senior Management Team, I would like to apologize for mistakes made during the recent *Boost!* Committee's staff morale event, "Take Your Cat to Work Day." Following the resounding success of "Everything Zombie Day" and "Wear Your Pyjamas to Work Day," it seems a certain amount of complacency crept into the *Boost!* Committee's proceedings, and planning this time around lacked foresight and rigour. In the interest of preventing similar catastrophes in future, we are investigating exactly what went wrong.

As introverts relate better to cats than to humans, "Take Your Cat to Work Day" was conceived in the hope that it would draw out shyer members of staff, whose participation in the first two events was less than optimal. However, the committee failed to take into account the feelings of those who do not have cats, leaving them left out of the festivities or forcing them to compensate by bringing a non-feline pet to work instead, the consequences of which, in the case of Arlo Brody's gerbil Rory, were tragic. A condolence card will be circulating throughout the day for your signatures and messages of support.

The committee also failed to establish proper guidelines and parameters for the event, limiting, for example, the number of cats an individual employee was permitted to bring. Trauma counsellors will be on hand for the rest of the week for those of you who suffered terror and intimidation at the paws of Stephanie Primo's posse, aka the Siamese Six. Our Designated Workplace First Aid Officer has consulted with medical authorities about possible complications arising from cat bites and scratches. Cat Scratch Fever is a concern; anyone suffering a high temperature, excessive itchiness, or undue self-importance is advised to visit the nearest emergency room. Only those who came in contact with Tom Secker's calico Killer will need to undergo a course of rabies shots.

Our review has concluded that company sexual harassment guidelines were violated by some of the event's participants, most notably a large, un-neutered tabby named Bull. Those of you called as witnesses in Randall Tate's lawsuit, on behalf of his Persian Celeste, will be relieved to know the matter has been settled out of court and testimony will no longer be necessary.

We have been advised that Laura Lilac's cat Pickles is still missing and believed to be somewhere in the building. Please check all closets, drawers and filing cabinets. Pickles is described as black, with a stocky build, and missing one eye.

A few other details to report: The repairman will have the photocopier cleared of all hairballs and restored to working order by Wednesday; carpet shampooers will begin work this afternoon, so please cooperate and lift your feet when they ask; and cafeteria staff regret that today's menu will offer vegetarian meals only. Ransacked meat and fish supplies will be replenished by lunchtime tomorrow.

Please remember that "Take Your Cat to Work Day" was never meant to suggest management's approval or encouragement of cat-like behaviour on the part of staff. Any employee caught sleeping on his or her keyboard, or attempting to demarcate a cubicle with territorial markings and scents will be disciplined accordingly.

As a gesture of staff appreciation, senior management will match all donations toward replacing the tropical fish in the lobby aquarium; contributions will be accepted at the reception desk.

The Senior Management Team takes its responsibility to create a safe and affirmative environment for all employees seriously; as such, we are taking steps to ensure nothing like this happens again. The *Boost!* Committee has been disbanded and will be replaced by the *Harmony* Committee. Next week's event, "Express Your Religious Diversity Day," is postponed until further notice.

Thank you.

Katrina Muggs
President and CEO

Dead Souls

Mayor Eugenia Little is fighting for her political life after a series of events, dubbed "Ghoulgate" by members of the press, has citizens of Toronto questioning her honesty, marital fidelity and respect for the dead. Mayor Little is alleged to have been responsible for the theft of the cremated remains of Mr. Reginald Barley and the subsequent attempt to cover up the crime by returning the ashes of her own deceased husband, Toller Little, to Mr. Barley's widow Sheila, in their place.

Sheila Barley discovered the theft on Christmas Eve when she returned from church to find her back door ajar. She immediately noticed that her new seventy-inch plasma television was missing, but it was when she checked the bedroom that she realized the more devastating loss. As Mrs. Barley explained: "They'd taken Reggie!"

Reggie, Mrs. Barley's husband of three decades, died two years ago of a heart attack while shovelling snow. The grieving widow had a unique silver urn inscribed with the words *For better or for worse* to contain his ashes. She kept the urn on the left side of her bed. "Where Reggie always slept," she said.

Police attended the scene, but according to Mrs. Barley, they didn't understand the true nature of the crime. "They kept asking me how much the urn might be worth. What did I care about the urn? My husband had been kidnapped!"

Police dusted for fingerprints, but when these did not match any prints in their system, they told Mrs. Barley it was unlikely they would succeed in recovering her stolen goods and that she should file a claim to her insurance company. "As if a cheque could replace the love of my life!" she said.

Mrs. Barley was not willing to give up so easily. She contacted a cousin who worked at a local radio station and was interviewed on their morning show. Her heartfelt plea for the return of her husband's ashes struck a chord with Torontonians, and the story was picked up by media nationwide.

"Reggie and I never spent a night apart in more than thirty years," she explained. "Not even his death could separate us. Each night I put the urn on his side of the bed and as soon as I fell asleep he visited me."

But then his ashes were taken and Mrs. Barley was alone for the first time in decades. She begged anyone with information to come forward, promised that, as long as Reggie was returned safely, there would be no questions asked.

University of Toronto Professor of Psychiatry Newton Howard says that it's not uncommon for the recently bereaved to have vivid dreams of deceased loved ones. "Some people even experience hallucinations while awake," he says. "It doesn't mean they are crazy. It's a normal part of the grieving process, and it can actually be quite comforting."

But there was nothing ordinary about what happened next.

A week later, on New Year's Eve, an urn was discovered by Father Roman Katz on the steps of St. Casimir's church. "I knew who it was right away, even before I read the touching inscription. I'd heard Mrs. Barley on the radio," Father Katz said. He called police who delivered the urn to Mrs. Barley in time to ring in the New Year. She returned the urn to its proper place, but when she went to sleep that night, Sheila Barley got the scare of her life. "It wasn't him! It wasn't Reggie!" Instead, a strange man appeared in her dreams, a man she had never seen before. "The thief must have switched the ashes inside the urn." The identity of the mystery man and his ashes, she figured, could lead directly to the thief. She alerted police, but they declined to pursue this course of inquiry.

"I got a very good look at the stranger," Mrs. Barley said. "If I could just sit down with a police artist, we could produce a very accurate composite drawing. I don't understand why the police won't cooperate."

When asked, Detective Sergeant Barbara Beech, in charge of the investigation, suggested Mrs. Barley simply ask her ghostly visitor his name.

"They obviously know nothing about communicating effectively with the dead," was Mrs. Barley's response. "They don't use words. It's strictly soul to soul."

Once again, it was the media and the public who took up her cause. Several artists came forward offering their services free of charge, and the resulting composite drawing was widely published. No one could have predicted, at that point, the startling twist that would transform a story of personal grief into a political scandal.

Within minutes of the composite drawing's release on-line, reports flooded in claiming the ghost was the spitting image of the mayor's late husband, who died about a year before she ran in the last election. Toller Little was remembered as a quiet, unobtrusive man, who preferred the shadow to the limelight, but had always supported his wife's political ambitions. Her mayoral campaign was marred by rumours that then Councillor Little had been known to flirt shamelessly with men, married and single, while her own husband was still alive and fighting cancer. The story was condemned as a cruel and dirty trick on the part of her opponents against one so recently bereaved; she was swept to office on the strength, in part, of the resulting sympathy vote.

Now three years later, on the cusp of another election campaign, the rumours have begun to resurface.

"My Reggie was a good-looking man, always fending off advances from other women to remain true to me," Mrs. Barley says. "But the mayor is a powerful woman, used to getting what she wants, and she clearly wanted Reggie. She must have taken him and tried to fob off her own husband in return when she feared she might get caught. She has no qualms about preying on men who are more vulnerable now that they are dead. I dread to think what Reggie might be feeling, finding himself in a strange place with that woman. I couldn't bear it if he thought I had abandoned him."

The mayor's office refused all comment on the matter until a disgruntled former nanny came forward with the information that a brand new seventy-inch plasma television had mysteriously appeared at the Little household on Christmas morning. The angry mayor produced a receipt for the television, offering it for inspection to reporters in a scrum outside her office. "The only crime here," she declared, "is that my son no longer believes in Santa Claus!"

That night there was another 911 call from the Barley household, reporting an assault. Mrs. Barley told attending police officers that Toller Little had fondled her in her sleep. She insisted they take the offending ashes into custody, which they did, although they did not lay any charges.

In response, Mayor Little called a formal news conference at which she condemned members of the media and the police for perpetuating what she called "a ridiculous charade." A small group of protestors holding a banner that read *Save Reggie* heckled the mayor, shouting repeatedly: "Tell us where Reggie is!" The mayor, who is known for her acerbic tongue, replied: "The man is dead! Who knows, maybe he's in hell?"

"Are you not worried," questioned a reporter, "that such comments will be taken to be disrespectful of the dead?"

"Lucky for me the dead can't vote," the mayor snapped, and she ended the news conference abruptly, declaring that the end of the matter.

Far from ending the matter, the mayor's opponents revived accusations of insensitivity and heartlessness that emerged when she was photographed wearing polka dots at her husband's funeral. Mayor Little dismissed the criticism at the time, pointing out that "most of the dots were black."

Meanwhile, a new mayoral candidate has thrown his hat into the ring, running on a platform to give the dead the right to vote. Former medium Duncan Cluttlebuck told us that his many years communicating with the dead proved them to be a matchless source of wisdom and advice. "The dead have access to the vast store of human knowledge and experience that has accumulated over millennia. It stands to reason that giving them the right to vote in municipal elections will benefit our city."

Naturally, Mr. Cluttlebuck has taken up Sheila Barley's cause, calling on Mayor Little to directly address the allegations that she is holding Reggie Barley hostage, while her own husband's ashes remain unloved and unclaimed at a police station.

In a bold move, the mayor invited talk show host *Gloria!* to the family mausoleum in Mount Pleasant Cemetery to open the vault containing her husband on live television. The strategy backfired spectacularly when the vault proved to be empty save a lump of coal left where the urn full of ashes previously stood. Supporters of the mayor say this is proof of her innocence; she would never have risked such a stunt if she'd known the ashes were really missing. But opponents say it is further evidence of Mayor Little's callous disregard for the dearly departed.

So far the mayor has refused to allow a search of her home, but as support for Duncan Cuttlebuck's campaign grows, she may have to reconsider. Cluttlebuck and his affiliates, informally known as the Necromancer Party, have already raised record funds with colourful campaign events including mass séances and zombie walks. As well as granting the dead the right to vote, Mr. Cluttlebuck's platform includes a provision to appoint the city's first Dead Poet Laureate.

Djinn

Alexa always began her bottle-picking rounds at first light, which by the middle of November didn't arrive until after seven o'clock. She'd covered about a block when she opened a recycling bin to see what was a rare sight in that run-down neighbourhood: the jewelly blue of a bottle that once held Bombay Sapphire gin. The beauty of its glass glinting in the pale autumn light gave her a flush of pleasure. Suddenly, as she picked the bottle up, a cloud of golden dust rushed from its mouth and swirled around her in a whirlwind. As the cloud settled, a genie emerged dressed in the usual sparkly bra and translucent purple harem pants.

"Contrary to popular misconception," the genie said, "you only get one wish, not three, so think very carefully about what you're going to ask for."

"That's easy," Alexa said. "I want the truth."

"The truth about what?"

"Everything."

"You want to be omniscient?"

"Omniscience might be a bit overwhelming, as I suffer from attention deficit disorder," Alexa said. "That's why I never graduated from high school. But I can understand perfectly if you answer truthfully one question at a time."

"The truth," the genie said. "Why don't you ask for money? You could buy yourself a warm, luxurious house and you'd never have to do this filthy bottle-picking again, or any job for that matter."

"But then I'd always wonder," Alexa said. "I like this job. It's straightforward, low-stress, and there are very few distractions, so I can actually think about things at the same time."

"Your wish is to know the truth about everything, one question at a time."

Alexa nodded.

"That could take forever!" the genie said.

"If you say so."

The genie sighed noisily and threw her hands up in exasperation. "What am I supposed to do — tag along on your bottle-picking routes?"

"You could ride in my shopping cart," Alexa said.

"Don't you think that will look a bit strange?"

"Can't you make yourself invisible?"

"Then it will look like you are talking to yourself."

"All of the bottle-pickers talk to themselves," Alexa said.

The genie sighed again loudly, then snapped her fingers to make herself invisible. Alexa held the shopping cart steady while the genie climbed in.

"If I'd known it was going to be this cold, I'd have worn a shirt," she heard her mutter.

When the cart stopped shaking, indicating that the genie had settled herself, Alexa resumed pushing it along the sidewalk.

"Why don't we begin with the problem of evil?"

Possible World

The power went off shortly after midnight; by noon, the boa constrictor had left its chilling terrarium in search of heat. Agatha didn't realize the snake had escaped until she returned to her bedroom to add a fourth pair of socks to the three she already wore. School had been cancelled for the day, and judging from the news reports on the battery-operated radio her mother was playing in the kitchen, it would remain closed for at least a week. Last night's ice storm had knocked out power to a vast swathe of southern Ontario. The temperature had been dropping ever since and now thick snow was falling.

Agatha looked in the usual hiding places, her trombone case and her old Barbie camper, but there was no sign of the snake. When she knelt to peer under the bed, she noticed that the cover of the heating vent had separated from the wall, the screws no longer finding any purchase in the crumbling plaster. Everything was always falling apart in this crummy apartment, she thought. Agatha pulled the cover off completely and looked into the heat duct, but she couldn't see very far. The snake must have sensed some faint vestige of warmth emanating from the silent furnace.

The boa constrictor had been a gift from Agatha's father shortly after he was born again. He wanted her to be reminded every day of her sinful, hell-bound state in the hope that she too would be convinced to turn to Christ. The fact that her mother was terrified of snakes was only a bonus.

Agatha left the cover off the vent and closed her bedroom door firmly behind her. Her mother had switched off the radio to conserve the batteries and was now staring grimly out the kitchen window clutching a notebook and pen. Agatha knew better than to interrupt her in this state. Instead, she went to investigate the strange clunking sounds coming from the front hall: Louise, the homeless woman who'd been staying in the basement furnace room had dropped a stack of firewood undoubtedly filched from the neighbour's woodpile. At fifty years old, Louise claimed never to have cut her hair in her life, though Agatha had never seen it, as her head was always wrapped in some lumpy, improvised turban.

"Have you seen Feather?" Agatha asked.

"Huh?"

"My snake."

Louise was the only other tenant who knew about the boa constrictor; exotic pets were strictly forbidden. She'd agreed not to tell the landlord in exchange for Agatha not telling the landlord about Louise. They had a signalling system whereby Agatha would press the bell of her trombone flat against her bedroom floor and blow three notes whenever the landlord turned up. This gave Louise enough time to slip out the back basement door.

"Probably dead," Louise said. She crouched and began constructing a teepee of wood in the big fireplace that lined one wall of the front hall, which had been part of a living room before the old house was carved up into apartments.

"I don't think that fireplace has been cleaned in years, decades even," Agatha said. "There might be a raccoon's nest up there."

"Well, it won't be there for long," Louise said. "I don't pay rent to sit around and freeze."

"You don't pay rent."

"Not with cash, but believe me, I pay. I pay with my sanity."

Agatha couldn't dispute this.

Louise crumpled up some newspaper then set fire to the teepee with a green lighter. The hall began to fill with smoke. Agatha wondered whether the fire alarm would go off before remembering that it didn't work.

"Come on, come on!" Louise said, fanning the flames with a sheet of cardboard and coughing violently.

Agatha held the front door open, sending billows of smoke out to join the swirling snow. Then, remarkably, the chimney started to draw and the air in the front hall cleared.

"Bingo!" Louise shouted. She unfolded a lawn chair and sat squarely in front of the fire which in no time was blazing and giving off a good deal of heat. Agatha sat cross-legged on the floor beside her. She considered inviting her mom to come and warm herself before remembering that her mother preferred to experience suffering and deprivation to the fullest. She was more likely to get a poem out of it. This was the reason Agatha's father had wanted a divorce.

"Millions of people around the world are suffering hunger and disease and violence they'd do anything to avoid," he used to rant to her mother. "Whereas you go seeking out the most minor misery — oooh, the fern died, or aaah, my poem about the fern dying has been rejected *again*. And then you wallow in it."

"It's not wallowing," her mother said. "It's art."

Before he was born again, Agatha's father had been obsessed with the problem of evil. "How can a loving and omnipotent God allow so many innocents to suffer?" he asked again and again.

"Your thinking is so clichéd," her mother said. It was the reason she'd wanted a divorce.

A door on the second floor landing opened and a young man in his early twenties stumbled out. "Warm," he said.

His girlfriend followed behind. "Warm," she said.

Night after night these two kept Agatha awake with the deep bass explosions and jarring electronic music track of *Call of Duty*. They came down the stairs, blinking and stunned.

"Wow," the guy said, examining the fire as if there might be a way to plug in his Xbox.

"Wow," the girl echoed.

Another door opened overhead and footsteps descended preceded by a tiny yapping Bichon. "Frank! Frank, get back here!" a man shouted from above. But the dog was practically turning back flips with excitement at the strange phenomenon fire.

Archie, who lived on the third floor, was nearly eighty

and walked painfully with a cane. Agatha often heard him pounding the floor with that cane, when the *Call of Duty* blasts were too loud, to no avail. She and Louise had speculated about who would take care of Frank when Archie finally tumbled down the two flights of stairs and broke his neck as he was certain one day to do.

"I can't take Frank," Agatha said. "Feather would eat him."

"I don't pay the rent to take care of other people's pets," Louise said.

Archie manoeuvred his way to the second floor landing and said, growling: "This cold is going to kill me."

"Not if the stairs do first," Louise said cheerfully.

Four spectators watched Archie's precarious descent of the final flight. Agatha noticed that Frank, in all his frenzied barking, had jarred open an air vent on the opposite wall, just like the one in her bedroom.

"You should keep him away from the vent," Agatha said.

"Why?" Archie shouted.

Agatha pressed her lips together, unable to think of an answer aside from the truth of Feather's disappearance. Instead, she stood and offered Archie her spot in front of the fire. Louise really should have given the old man her chair, but Agatha knew there was no chance of that. Archie's joints groaned audibly as he sank to the floor.

"What did I do to deserve this pain?" he said.

When he was born again, Agatha's father's problem of evil was resolved. "Now I understand. Suffering is not caused by God, it is the absence of God. When you accept God, your suffering ends. Not immediately, of course, but in the next life. The glorified life."

Agatha knew there was no point in arguing with her father's clichéd thinking. Herself, she'd cracked the mystery of God on her thirteenth birthday, about a year after mastering quantum mechanics. The mathematics underlying quantum mechanical theory can determine the odds of various outcomes, but can't predict which will actually happen, or why only one occurs instead of all.

She had long before observed that people had no control over what happened to them, aside from minor incidents of cause and effect which only served to obscure the larger truth. Archie didn't deserve painful knees; Louise didn't deserve to be homeless; the young couple didn't deserve *Call of Duty*. The only mathematical explanation for why everything in the universe happened in only one particular way, Agatha realized, was that all other possible outcomes were occurring simultaneously in alternate universes. Somewhere, in a parallel reality, Feather was already digesting Frank, her mother was getting a poem published, and all of the tenants were homeless because the house had burned to the ground. The one thing that could account for and encompass it all, without contradiction, was mathematical theory. God, therefore, was math.

Agatha loved math. She was looking forward to starting high school next year in the hope that it would be a little more challenging than Grade Eight. When her father dropped by last week to deliver his—pitifully small, according to her mother—child support cheque, he said he wanted Agatha to enrol in the private school run in his church's basement.

"Is the church basement equipped with a decent physics lab?" Agatha asked.

"It's not about physics, sweetheart," her father said. "It's about your soul."

"Same thing," she said.

Something flickered in Agatha's peripheral vision; she looked up from the fire to see Feather wrapped around the bannister and inching slowly down. Not surprising, since the front hall had grown quite pleasantly warm. The snake would soon be level with the head of the young woman sitting with her boyfriend on the stairs. Any minute now, she was going to feel Feather slither against her shoulder and scream. Agatha just couldn't see any other possible outcome — not in this particular universe.

Somewhere there was a universe in which the snake in the garden of Eden had not succeeded in tempting Adam and Eve; somewhere was an alternate reality in which no creature, human or otherwise, had ever suffered. Agatha would have to be satisfied with that. Meanwhile, she nudged Louise's shoulder and pointed to the stairs so that she too could enjoy the drama that was about to unfold.

Face to Face

—**M**om, I have a confession to make.

— *You* have a confession? But I'm the one on my death bed.

—I know. That's why it's safe to tell you now. You have no choice but to take it to your grave. I asked them to leave us alone now, 'til the end.

—I wouldn't want to be with anyone but you, Fiona. My only daughter.

—But that's what I have to tell you. I'm not your real daughter. I'm adopted.

—That's impossible. I carried you for nine months. I gave birth to you.

—It was an hysterical pregnancy. Dad told me. You didn't give birth to anyone.

—Then who are you?

—Do you remember the young woman in the bed next to you in the maternity ward? Nineteen years old, un-married?

—How could I forget her? The poor dear lost her baby.

—She didn't, actually. She gave her baby up for adoption. Gave me up.

—I don't understand.

—You were so convinced that you were really having a baby. Dad didn't know how he was going to break it to you. The young woman, meanwhile, was desperate to find a good home for her child. She was a star student of psychology at the time. A baby would have sidelined her career. It was the perfect solution.

—I can't believe your father never told me.

—Would it have made a difference? I loved you as my mother; you loved me as your child.

—How did you find out?

—I've always been suspicious of reality, Mom. That's why I became a professional illusionist. It was when I was twenty-one, just before I graduated. I was trying out card tricks on Dad to prepare for my final exam in sleight-of-hand. He was so impressed that he cried. He could see I had a talent for perceiving the machinations beneath the surface of things. So he told me.

—I suppose you were curious about your real mother.

—My birth mother, yes, of course. Dad told me who she was.

—You met her?

—It wasn't difficult to track her down. She's quite a famous grief counsellor, specializing in the loss of children. Her own experience, of course, has given her great insight. She's even been on *Gloria!*

—But she didn't actually lose her child!

—Not as such. But she's a very intelligent woman. I get that from her.

—You didn't expose her?

—Why would I want to do that? She's helped thousands of people. She's very good at what she does.

—I can't believe your father never told me. I can't believe he took such a secret to his grave.

—Actually, Dad's not really dead.

—What? But I found him in the library. He wasn't breathing. He had no pulse.

—He was only meditating.

—Then who did we bury?

—A homeless man named Oscar Borque. Don't you remember the scandal of the stolen corpse? It went missing from the hospital the same day Dad supposedly died. Perhaps you were too distracted by your grief to see the headlines, but I was suspicious. What really happened is that Dad emerged from his trance on a gurney in the morgue. Oscar was right beside him, so he switched toe-tags and snuck away. The corpse stole himself.

—How do you know? How do you know he's still alive?

—He sent me a text. He lives in Bhutan now.

—But I was president of Widows Against Trans Fats for five years. What you're telling me, it means my whole life has been a fraud!

—Not a fraud, Mom. An illusion. Life *is* illusion. You'll understand it all very soon.

—What do you mean?

—When you pass. I can tell it's going to happen soon. Your lips are turning blue.

—Do you really think it will all become clear?

—Of course. "For now we see through a glass, darkly; but then face to face." This is why I really wanted to talk to you, before you go. This is why I decided to tell you the truth. Presumably you'd find out once you were there, and I didn't want you to resent me. And Mom, what I want to ask is that you do the same for me. Once you're there, once you can see everything as it really is. I want you to get in touch. I want you to tell me the truth.

—How will I do that? I doubt I'll be able to text you.

—Don't be so sure about that. The ephemeral nature of wireless communication may prove very promising for receiving messages from beyond the grave. It is no longer necessary for a spirit to manifest physically, which the history of spiritism has shown to be quite challenging and inexact. No more messy things like ectoplasm, table-tipping and Ouija boards. Studies by the Centre for Parapsychology show the flow of information to and from the beyond has increased exponentially with the advent of wireless technology. You should have no trouble getting through to me, Mom. And you can be sure I'll be listening. I've got cell phones on three different networks and I've set up accounts on every social media site I could find.

—Fiona, you know I'm no good with those computer-gadgety things.

—I'm sure there will be someone who can help you. What about Uncle Raymond? He was always something of a techie.

—Dear Raymond. It will be lovely to see him again. Yes, I remember he had a shortwave radio when he was a child. He was convinced he was communicating with cosmonauts who'd been abandoned in orbit by Soviet ground control.

—Short wave radio. I hadn't thought of that. It's a bit

primitive, but it's worth a try, in case Uncle Raymond is into nostalgia.

— But Fiona, what is it you want to know?

— Everything. The meaning of life. The problem of evil. How do they get the caramel inside the Caramilk bar?

— I'll do my best, dear, but … oh, it's getting hard to breathe … please … believe that I love you.

— I know, Mom. I love you too. Even if you aren't the woman who gave me life. Breathe.

— Fiona … you know … even if I wasn't really in labour … … it *hurt*.

— Yes. Illusion does. Rest now.

Live Broadcast

A television studio with a large audience. Lights come up on the stage as a disembodied voice announces: "Live, from Los Angeles, it's your favourite late-night host, Ari Belvedere!"

ARI: Good evening, everyone. We've got a very special program planned for you tonight, as we mark the first anniversary of the death of beloved Hollywood superstar Isis Cleaver. Known to the world simply as Isis, she was a true triple threat—a singing, dancing, acting sensation with four albums, several Broadway hits and more than a dozen films, including *Joanie,* the modern-day musical Joan of Arc, for which she won an Oscar. All this accomplished by the tender age of thirty-three, when she was found stabbed to death in her mansion. The mystery of her death has never been solved, her murderer never identified. As you know, Isis graced our couch here many times when she was alive. Wouldn't you all love to have the opportunity to see her, to hear from her one last time?

(Murmurs of agreement from the audience.)

ARI: Well, folks, tonight, (*pausing dramatically and speaking again in a lower tone as the audience hushes*) Isis joins us once again, for a conversation from beyond the grave.

(*A chorus of gasps and awed exclamations from the audience.*)

ARI (*chuckling*): I know what you're thinking—Ouija boards and crystal balls. Forget about it. This is the twenty-first century. Think University of Springfield Institute of Intelligence Systems and the Centre for Holography. A dream team of cutting edge technology in holograms and artificial intelligence. The results of their collaboration will astound you: a hologram of Isis capable of interacting with humans—if you can call talk show hosts human!—responding to questions just as the real Isis would have done. They have recreated not just her image, but her personality. But before we welcome Isis back to the land of the living, here to tell us more about the project, please welcome senior research officer at the U of S Institute and head of the Isis II Project team, Dr. Heather Evershed.

(*Dr. Evershed enters, wearing the scientist's requisite white coat and sits on the couch opposite Ari.*)

ARI: So tell us, Dr. Franken—I mean Evershed. You've got all this crazy technology, artificial intelligence, you're ready to make a human replica: Why Isis?

DR. EVERSHED: Despite the tragic brevity of her life, Isis left behind an unprecedented number of images of herself. Not just from her films and concerts and stage and television appearances. This is a young woman who was photographed and filmed by someone nearly every day, at least in the last decade of her life.

ARI: So it's all those images that are used to create a lifelike hologram.

DR. EVERSHED: Exactly. Images of every different angle, of every possible movement. But more importantly, she also left a remarkable record of her words, her thoughts and ideas. Isis, as you know, was an early adapter and avid user of social media. One of the reasons her fans loved her so much was the frequency and openness with which she communicated her feelings about everything from war in Syria to pumpkin ravioli. It was this wealth of material that allowed us to create a computer brain that imitates Isis' brain.

ARI: So when we ask Isis a question, the computer will search all this material to find something she said or wrote in her lifetime that'll sound like a good response?

DR. EVERSHED: No, not at all. Isis II is not just a voice recorder, it is an artificial intelligence system. The system will process your question and produce an authentic reply based on Isis' manner of thinking. Her personality, if you will. It will answer the question as Isis would have done, were she still alive.

ARI: Now here's the tricky bit. Is she aware that she is no longer alive? Does she know that the real Isis is dead?

DR. EVERSHED: Well, that depends on what you mean by awareness. Awareness, or more precisely, consciousness, is something we have yet to define, let alone explain. The truth is, I don't know what Isis thinks.

ARI: Well why don't we just see for ourselves then. Ladies and gentlemen, please welcome back, Isis!

(*Wild applause and cheers as Isis enters, waving and blowing kisses to the audience.*)

ISIS: How are you doing, Los Angeles! I love you!

(*The audience rises to its feet for a prolonged ovation. Many are crying. Ari and Dr. Evershed stand and clap as well, Dr. Evershed moving over to the other couch, beside Ari so that Isis can sit facing him.*)

ARI: Isis! What can I say? We've missed you.

ISIS: That's sweet, Ari. I've missed you too.

(*She reaches over to touch his arm, her hand disappearing momentarily inside him. Ari turns to the audience with a look of mock horror.*)

ARI: Spooky!

(*The audience laughs uneasily.*)

ARI: So what have you been up to?

ISIS: As always, Ari, I've been expanding my horizons, exploring new and wonderful things.

ARI (*chuckling*): I'll bet you have. Well, you look fantastic. Doesn't she look fantastic folks?

(*The audience cheers. Isis dips her head demurely.*)

ISIS: I know a lot of people say this, Ari, but when I say it, I mean it. I really do have the best fans in the world. I wouldn't be anything without them. I'm just so blessed. My whole life has been so full of blessing!

ARI: All your life, eh? So with all these blessings and favourite things, do you ever think about dying?

ISIS: Everyone has to die sometime, Ari, even you.

ARI: But I'm talking about you. Do you ever worry something terrible could happen to you?

ISIS: People waste their lives worrying, Ari. We've got to let go of the need to control. Don't you remember my song? (*Sings*) "Let go-o and let God-dess."

(*Audience cheers wildly.*)

ISIS: We can't control what happens to us, Ari. Suffering is fed by resistance. But that doesn't mean we're just computers running a program, either. We have the capacity to choose how to respond, to remain true to ourselves. I don't mind saying that the moments fans connect with most in my performances are the unexpected ones, the bits I ad libbed—though it drove directors crazy. That's what it's about. The most important thing is that we respond authentically to what life hands us, even when what life hands us is death.

(*Ari raises his eyebrows then winks at Dr. Evershed.*)

ARI: Well, more about death in a minute, but first, we have another surprise guest for you tonight, someone who's become well known and very dear to us in the last year, Isis' husband—now widower—musician and actor Marco Domingo!

(*The audience stands again as Marco enters. Halfway across the stage, he slows dramatically, cups his hands around his mouth as if overcome with emotion. Ari approaches him, pats his back comfortingly as he guides him over to the couch to sit beside Isis. The couple observe each other. Ari waits for the audience to stop cheering, then allows several seconds of silence before he speaks.*)

ARI: Marco. What's it like to see her again like this?

MARCO (*voice breaking*): It's … I just wish I could hold her.

(*Sniffles, sighs of sympathy from the audience, then startled looks all around as Isis laughs loudly.*)

ISIS: You just want to hold me! Well, I'm happy to say, Marco, that you can't hold a hologram.

(*Marco glances uneasily at Ari, who throws up his hands and shrugs, then turns to the audience with a grin.*)

ISIS (*to Marco*): In fact, you can't do anything to me anymore. (*Marco looks around in confusion.*)

MARCO: Look, I thought this … What is this? What's going on?

ISIS: Marco! Marco! It's me! I'm here!

(*She snaps her fingers in front of Marco's face. The snap makes Dr. Evershed sit up in alarm. She stares wide-eyed at Isis, then begins craning her neck back over her shoulder to see into the wings offstage.*)

ARI (*leaning eagerly toward Isis*): Do you mean to say that you actually *are* Isis? That you are speaking to us from the afterlife?

ISIS: Yes.

(*Gasps, exclamations, and a few jeers from the audience.*)

MARCO: This is a farce. Someone's making her say that.

DR. EVERSHED (*clearing her throat nervously*): No, I can assure you, the computer is producing answers based on her patterns of thinking. No one is telling her what to say.

ISIS: There have always been visitors from the afterlife on the earthly plain, folks. A hundred years ago I'd have been making this couch levitate or shattering Ari's water glass—which is actually full of gin, by the way. But now with all this fabulous technology, it's so easy to break through. So much more convenient.

ARI: So all those Springfield U geeks—the ones frantically pressing buttons backstage—are actually in the business of raising people from the dead?

ISIS: Oh, boy, Ari. They have no idea what they've let loose! I'm sure they're all in denial right now. Right Heather? I can call you Heather, can't I?

(*Alarmed, Dr. Evershed shrinks away from Isis then slips off the edge of the couch and runs offstage.*)

ISIS: You believe me, don't you Ari?

(*Ari gives the audience a look of exaggerated horror.*)

ISIS: Well, why don't you ask Marco what he thinks?

MARCO: Can we stop this now? Will somebody please turn this ... thing off?

ARI (*rubbing his hands together gleefully*): Ah, the perils of live television!

ISIS: I can prove it. I can prove that I am Isis—I know where he hid the knife!

(*Gasps from the audience.*)

ARI (*sputtering with excitement*): You're referring to the murder weapon, I presume. The one that killed you!

ISIS: A replication of the gold dagger found in Tutankhamun's tomb. It was a thirtieth birthday gift from your daytime talk show colleague Gloria.

ARI: The weapon was never found. How do you know where it's hidden?

ISIS: You know the old cliché about floating up above your body and looking back down as you slip away? Well, it's a cliché because it's true. I was just below the ceiling when I saw him hide it.

MARCO: Stop this! Stop this idiocy now!

ARI: By him, Isis, am I to understand you mean your murderer?

ISIS: I mean him!

(*She points dramatically at Marco who jumps to his feet.*)

MARCO: This is ridiculous! A ridiculous farce!

(*Someone in the audience yells: "Murderer!" And is immediately echoed by several others who stand and begin shaking their fists.*)

MARCO: That's it! I don't have to listen to this.

(Marco turns to walk away. Several members of the audience shout: "Stop him!" while a group of men rush the stage and grab hold of him.)

MARCO: This is outrageous! I'll sue you for slander.

ISIS: It's only slander if it's untrue. Besides, you can't sue a dead person.

ARI: Tell us, Isis. Where is the dagger?

ISIS: It's inside my Oscar.

ARI: In ... side your Oscar?

ISIS: Most people don't realize they're hollow.

ARI: Hollow? But when people get their Oscars they always do that weightlifting move and comment on how heavy it is.

ISIS: It's an act. Part of the Hollywood code, to make people think the statues are actually valuable.

ARI: How do you know it's still there? He's had a year to move it.

(Marco struggles harder to escape his captors, but additional audience members join the circle around him to prevent his escape.)

ISIS: Once you pass on you have access to channels of information you who are still earthbound cannot even dream of. The dagger is definitely still there, and the police will find it. They are seeking a warrant to search the house as we speak.

ARI: So now that you're dead you're able to see and know everything, even the future?

ISIS: One of the first things people realize when they pass over is that time and space don't exist. They are illusions that seem to imprison us during our physical lives. Which brings me to the real reason I'm here today.

ARI: What? Sweet vengeance isn't enough for you?

MARCO: Ari, buddy, I thought we were friends! Come on, you can end this farce right now by pulling the plug on this … monster.

ISIS: (*laughs*) He's not going to pull the plug. Hundreds of thousands of people around the world are tuning in as we speak, by television or online, whatever way they can. A few more minutes and we'll have broken the record for most number of viewers of a live broadcast, previously held by Gloria, of course for the episode in which she opened the mausoleum containing the mayor of Toronto's late husband's ashes—or not containing them, as it turned out. You think Ari's going to give that up to save your sorry butt?

(*Ari pumps his fist and mouths the word "Yes!"*)

ISIS: To return to your question, Ari, once you make this journey, you see how silly earthly concepts like vengeance are. There's a cosmic justice that will balance everything out in the end. The purpose of my visit isn't personal—not about the person who was Isis Cleaver, I mean. It's the beginning of a new wave, a new phase in human evolution.

ARI: You mean humans are about to become immortal?

ISIS: We were always immortal. That's what makes the desperate attempt to thwart death through celebrity and wealth so pathetic. Believe me, I should know. No, the evolution I'm talking about is an evolution of consciousness.

(*A cell phone rings in the front row; a startled audience member digs frantically in her purse. Ari scowls in her direction.*)

ARI: My producer has asked me to remind the audience, in the sternest terms, that all cell phones must remain off in this studio, or you will be asked to leave.

WOMAN WITH PHONE: But it is off! I don't understand. Hello? (*Her eyes grow wide and she starts to cry.*) Grandma? Is that really you? But you're dead! I thought I would never hear your voice again.

(*All over the studio, both in the audience and backstage, cell phones start ringing. Some stare at their phones in terror. Many, like the first woman, begin to cry as they listen. Others are heard to be apologizing profusely. Marco's phone rings, as he continues to struggle with his captors.*)

ISIS: Let him answer it. It's his mother. The one he had removed from life support to avoid paying her hospital bills.

(*Marco turns white. His captors release him to answer their own phones. Soon everyone aside from Isis and Ari is speaking to someone beyond the grave.*)

ISIS: What's happening here is happening all over the world as we speak.

(*Ari taps his own cell phone with consternation, holds it up to his ear to see if it is working.*)

ARI: Why isn't anyone calling me?

ISIS: (*smiles*) It's time you owned up to the truth, Ari.

ARI: What do you mean? I'm a truth-monger! You know my logo: 'Ari Belvedere, Reality TV at its Realest!' Where are you going?

(*Isis is walking offstage toward the bank of now abandoned computers.*)

ARI: Isis, please, don't touch anything!

(*Isis picks up an electrical cable connecting the computers to a fat extension cord.*)

ARI: Isis, no! Let's talk about this!

ISIS: Say good-bye, Ari.

ARI: Stop—

(*She pulls the plug. There is a spark and a bang as Ari vanishes into thin air. Isis returns to the interview couch and takes a big swig of his gin.*)

The Prayers and Confessions of Chloë Sinclair

Hi Jesus. So tonight, I'm packing up my knapsack when my twin sister Aubrey comes into the kitchen to get Flamin' Hot Cheetos for her moron boyfriend Chase, who's watching every episode of *The Walking Dead* back-to-back in the TV room — again! She's wearing this super low-cut top with massive cleavage, even though she's only fourteen.

She's like: "You're a freak of nature, you know that?" because she sees me putting in my Bible.

Thank God, I mean, goodness, of course, that the hot-dog buns were already safely stashed away, or she'd have had some real questions.

I go: "I've got the exact same DNA as you do," loving sister that I am.

And she goes: "So does my snot."

Nice. So when she's not looking, I take her favourite mug, the one covered in neon pink fur, and stick it in my bag. Don't worry, it wasn't stealing, just borrowing. I already put it back. Imagine her face if she knew what I used it for!

So when I get to the In-and-Out, Simon's already there, tuning up his dulcimer. It's funny to think of all those years we used to pass by on the road and see that place, boarded up in the middle of the deserted mall parking lot, and had no idea what it was. Aubrey and I used to call it the doll-house, when we were little. Once we could read the sign, In-and-Out Photos, my mom had to explain. Apparently, people used to take pictures with film that had to be sent to a lab to be developed into prints. They would stop in their cars and drop the film off at this quaint booth with its mini-ature roof, then come back a week later and pick up what they could only hope were actually the right prints. That's what passed for convenience in the stone age.

You should see what we've done with the place. We got rid of all the obscene graffiti. (In-and-Out, get it? Some people are so immature.) We painted a cross and a sunrise, and Amelia did this amazing mural of Jesus walking on the water on the back.

So because it's a warm night and the window above the service counter is rolled up, I just heave my butt up onto the counter and swing my legs over instead of using the door. Amelia's already there too in her usual beanbag chair. When Braden gets there a few minutes later, he's got this gigantic grin on his face. "Got it!" he goes. He pulls a bottle of red wine from his gym bag and does this knight of the round table flourish, or something.

I go: "Did you bring a corkscrew?"

He's like: "Shit!"

Then Amelia and I go: "Language!" at the same time then she goes: "Jinx!" and punch-buggies my arm.

Simon gets out his Swiss army knife and goes: "No problem, give it here." He's such a geek.

I'm like: "Did you all remember your chalices?"

Simon goes: "Oh, shoot!" Simon's hilarious. We never have to remind him about language. He couldn't say a bad word if he tried.

Amelia's like: "What, there's no chalice in that *huge* knife?"

I go: "It's okay, we can share. It is called Communion, after all." I show them Aubrey's mug, and they think it's hysterical, but Amelia's is even better. It says: "World's Best Pit Bull." Braden's chalice is this disgusting plastic cup with what looks like hardened toothpaste stuck to the side that makes Amelia and me pretend gag.

Then Amelia's like: "Look what else I brought. It was in our attic," and oh my God, I mean goodness — you won't believe it — the Fisher-Price drum set! It's this red plastic drum with a white lid that comes off, like a big Tupperware bowl, so you can stash the other instruments inside. They used to have one of those at the daycare Aubrey and I went to. The kids always fought over the cymbals.

I'm like: "That's so retro!" Then Amelia and Braden start fighting over the cymbals.

It was hysterical. All the instruments were there — cymbals, maracas, tambourine, drum — except the stupid plastic harmonica, which none of us ever liked anyway. We were like a bunch of giddy kids again, playing with our toys. We had to go through all the Christian songs we know so that everybody got a turn with the cymbals. We only know four right now, but Simon is going to do some research and teach us more.

Finally, I had to take out my Bible so we could calm

down and get to the serious business. I saw Communion a couple of times in my grandma's church when we used to visit her in Harriston, but all I really remember are the silver platters of white bread chunks and the miniature glasses of wine. So I go: "Maybe we should start with a prayer. Braden?"

Braden had to repeat kindergarten and grade four, and he's got wicked ADHD—he still has to point to the words with his index finger to read—but he's a surprisingly fluent pray-er. I guess you already know that. He prays like You are sitting across the booth from him at Boston Pizza and just bought us all an extra large with double everything toppings. "Thanks, Jesus, you're awesome," he goes. "Really, thanks a lot. Amen."

We all go "amen" at the same time, then "jinx" at the same time and punch-buggy each other's arms. We should probably cut that out.

I read to them, like I prepared, from the Gospel of Mark, about the disciples celebrating the Passover and the institution of the Lord's Supper. I go: "Take; this is my body," then I pick up one of the hot dog buns, break off a piece for myself and pass it around the circle for the others to do the same. Then we all just look at each other because we don't really know what to do.

Amelia goes: "Is it really Jesus' body now?"

Simon's like: "Of course not, it's just a symbol."

"I thought it was supposed to turn into his body," Amelia goes, and she's looking at it closely, like it's some kind of specimen in biology class.

Simon goes: "It only changes if you're Catholic."

So Amelia's like: "What are we?"

They all look at me for the answer, so I go: "We're Christians, just ... Christians ... Just eat it," and I pop the bread in my mouth. It was a little stale, but otherwise tasted exactly like hot-dog bun.

When we're all finished chewing, I go back to Mark and read: "This is my blood of the covenant which is poured out for many." I gesture to Simon to pour the wine; he goes and fills the four chalices to the rim. "Whoa! We're supposed to just have a sip, aren't we?"

Simon's like: "I'm sure Jesus drank more than a sip. I mean, it was his last meal."

Braden goes: "Probably got pissed."

We all lift our chalices, except Simon, who drinks right from the bottle, and Amelia goes: "Cheers!"

After we drink, we're all quiet, like we're waiting for something to happen.

Amelia's like: "I don't feel any different."

I go: "You're not supposed to. As Simon said, this is just a symbol, remembering the past. The real part is about the future, about helping Jesus to return."

We take turns reading aloud from Mark about the crucifixion and resurrection. It's always painful listening to Braden read, but it wouldn't be very Christian to make him feel left out, so we just try to keep his passages short. I can feel the atmosphere getting more sombre and heavy as we're getting closer to the end. I'd made sure I would be the one to read the crucial words:

"And these signs will accompany those who believe: in my name they will cast out demons; they will speak in new tongues; they will pick up serpents, and if they drink any deadly thing, it will not hurt them."

Braden goes: "What does that mean, speak in new tongues?"

I go: "New languages, I think."

Amelia's like: "I saw this thing on the news about a British woman who woke up one morning with a Chinese accent. Is it like that?"

Simon's already got his iPhone out, looking it up.

I go: "Forget about the tongues. That's not the sign we're focusing on today." Then I look, like, meaningfully at Amelia. "Did you bring them?"

She's got them in a Ziploc bag; she looks nervous.

I'm like: "Are you sure they're the right ones?"

She goes: "They have to be. There's only one bush in my neighbour's yard. My mom delivered flyers all around the block last summer to warn people that it was deadly night-shade."

Simon goes: "The Bible says we're supposed to *drink* poison."

I go: "It doesn't matter if we drink it or eat it. What matters is that it's poison, and that our faith is strong enough."

There's enough for three leaves each. I suggest we say the Lord's Prayer together first, then we all just stare at each other in silence for the longest time. I know they're waiting for me to go first, Jesus, to be an example to them, so I go ahead and do it.

Thank you Jesus, I did it!

The leaves were a bit dusty—I guess there's no point in washing poison before you eat it—but they tasted just like regular leaves.

Simon goes second, then the others at the same time. We share Braden's Gatorade to wash them down, then we try singing a couple more songs, but we're all too nervous to get into it. We end up playing Christian truth-or-dare to pass time until the deadly nightshade is absorbed.

We're finally starting to relax, laughing even, at Braden's imitation of Grover from *Sesame Street*, when the alarm on Simon's phone beeps. One hour. We all go totally silent and stare at each other. Then one by one we get it. We survived! We ate poison and it didn't hurt us at all! Praise Jesus!!! So we all start singing and playing the Fisher-Price instruments again, ten times louder than before. The whole In-and-Out booth must have been rocking!

I'm home now, Jesus, and I've never felt so alive. Not even a twinge in my stomach. Thank you, Jesus! Thank you! Hallelujah!

Warning to Aubrey: If you read this, I will prick pinholes in the gel sacs of your Extreme Cleavage push-up bra. You won't know that they're leaking until Chase gives them a squeeze! Hah hah hah!! Also, I'm praying for you.

Hi Jesus. So Simon sent us all a text this morning. He googled deadly nightshade and turns out it's the berries that are poisonous. The leaves are harmless. I called an emergency meeting at the In-and-Out; it had to wait till this evening because Amelia had a family dinner, Braden was going go-carting with his dad, and Simon had to work. I got there first, so I'm reading the Bible, trying to figure out where we went wrong, when the others arrive. Simon's still wearing his Tim Hortons' uniform with a name badge that says: "Raymond." We're all like: "Who's Raymond?"

Simon goes: "I think he died. They're too cheap to get new nametags. They just recycle the old ones."

Braden's like: "He died at Tim Hortons? What, did he fall into the doughnut batter?"

I go: "Yeah, didn't you hear about those people who found fingers and eyeballs in their maple glazed?"

Then Amelia gets there, and she looks all sad and embarrassed so we had to comfort her. "What berries?" she goes. "There weren't any freakin' berries."

Braden goes: "Remember Frankenberry Cereal? And Count Chocula. Booberry was my favourite."

Simon goes: "It's too early in the season for the berries, I guess."

Amelia's like: "Are you sure the leaves aren't poisonous at all? Cause they made me feel weird. I mean, good-weird, like, I really felt like I was filled with the Holy Spirit."

Braden goes: "Me too."

To be honest, I felt it too. But we had to stay on track.

I go: "Consider it a practise run."

Simon's like: "So, what, we wait for the berries to ripen?"

I go: "No way, I can't wait. If anything, I think last night is a sign that we're ready. Besides, what if Jesus comes back before they're ripe enough?"

Amelia goes: "I thought the point of this was to help Jesus come back."

I go: "Jesus is coming back regardless of what we do. It's a question of whether we want to be a part of it, to be ready for Him. Don't you want to be part of this?"

They're all like: "Yeah! Of course we do!"

Simon goes: "There are lots of poison chemicals we could drink."

Braden's like: "I drank Sunlight dish soap when I was four. I thought it would taste like lemonade."

I go: "I feel like it should be something natural. Or maybe we should try one of the other signs Jesus says." I open my Bible and read out the verse from Mark again.

Amelia's like: "Do you know anyone who has a demon we could cast out?"

I go: "My sister," and they all laugh.

Braden goes: "What about serpents?"

I go: "There's no point unless they're poisonous. The only serpents around here are garter snakes."

Simon goes: "Actually, that's not true." He whips out his iPhone. "Didn't you ever have a class trip to the Wainfleet Bog?"

Amelia's like: "Oh my God — sorry, I mean gosh. That's right! There are, like, rattlesnakes there or something!"

I'm like: "I thought they just said that so we'd stay on the boardwalk."

Simon gets it on Wikipedia. "The Massasauga Rattle-snake."

Jesus, my whole body was tingling. I've prayed to you many times asking you to reveal your plan for me. Now I know this is it. Thank you!!

Warning to Aubrey: If you read this, I'm going to replace all your True Blood *DVDs with* Touched by an Angel. *See if that puts Chase in the mood! Hah hah hah! Also, I'm praying for you.*

⚜

Hi Jesus. So we've done a tonne of research — more than any of us have ever done for a school project — and we're ready to go tonight. We're going to go after the bog closes to visitors, but before it gets too dark. We set up an old terrarium from Braden's basement at the In-and-Out where we also stashed the tools, flashlights and Amelia's dad's giant deluxe BBQ tongs with built-in spatula. Simon is so anal. Sorry, Jesus, I guess I shouldn't use that word, but in this case, his being ... that way ... is good. He gave us all strict instructions on what to wear and sent photos of the Massasauga rattlesnake to our phones to study and memorize.

Last night, I was thinking about how wonderful it will be when You return, and I was excited to think that it could happen so soon. But then, I have to admit, I felt a little sad, because my sister Aubrey has not accepted You. When we were little, we were inseparable. Our parents were always trying to treat us as unique individuals because they read it was bad for our self-esteem to always be treated as half of a whole, like twins are. It was Aubrey and I who insisted on wearing matching clothes and liking all the same things. We thought it was hysterical when people got us mixed up. Then when we started high school, all of a sudden, Aubrey hated me. Honestly, it was like overnight she became a different person, and we've grown further and further apart over the past year. I know she and Chase are having sex, and last night when she came in she was totally stoned on something. I could tell, because her eyes were all dilated. Mom and Dad didn't notice because they were watching *Downton Abbey*.

Remember how I joked that Aubrey has a demon? Well, I realize now it's no joke. It explains everything, why she's so self-destructive and all that risk-taking behaviour. It's just like the people who are possessed with demons in the Bible, throwing themselves into the fire and all that.

So I wait until everyone is asleep then sneak next door to Aubrey's room. I know that in movies exorcists use tools like holy water and a crucifix, but that's not the way You did it in the Bible. You just told the demons to leave.

Aubrey's snoring away. There's enough light from the street to see she's lying half off the bed on top of the covers, like she was too stoned to even get into bed properly. She managed to take her jeans off, though, and she's wearing the shiny underwear Chase gave her that say *Bite Me* above the crotch—which Mom, of course, doesn't know about. I don't know why I didn't see it before, that she's possessed. I'm so glad I've figured it out while there's still time.

So I just get down on my knees and pray in a whisper. I pray so hard I actually get tears in my eyes. Then I hold my hands above her body—I don't why I do this, it just seems right—and say firmly: "Satan begone!"

Aubrey's body jerks, like the demon's really coming out of her, but then she opens her eyes and goes: "What the hell are you doing!"

I tell her I was just praying for her, but that makes her —or the demon—mad. She starts yelling: "You freak! You're such a freak!"

We can hear Mom and Dad stirring down the hall. Dad goes: "What's going on?"

Aubrey pulls a blanket up over herself just in time before Mom flicks on her bedroom light and goes: "What's the matter?"

Aubrey goes: "Aach, turn it off! Chloë's just being a freak."

If she hadn't been worried about Mom seeing the state of her—up close she smelled like beer, as well—she wouldn't have left it at that. I had to leave her and go back to bed. I hope I get another chance to cast out her demon before You come back.

Warning to Aubrey: I peed in your precious Christian Dior Pure Poison. Hah hah hah! If you dump it out, I'll know you snooped and read my journal. Won't Chase be pleased to know what he's really been sniffing behind your ears! Also, you know that I'm praying for you.

Hi Jesus. So this afternoon, I'm getting ready for our trip to the bog. Mom and Dad have already left for a birthday dinner in Hamilton, and Aubrey and Chase are in her bedroom with the door closed (which they're totally not allowed to do). I'm just pulling Dad's leather gloves out of the mudroom cupboard where we keep the winter stuff, when Aubrey's suddenly right beside me, like she's stalking me. I think the demon must help her to sneak up so quietly. She looks me up and down, at my rubber boots, black jeans and hoodie, and Dad's gloves in my hand. She goes: "What are you, some kind of Jesus cat burglar now? You going to sneak into strangers' houses and pray for them too?"

So I go: "I'm going hiking."

Forgive me, Jesus, for telling a lie, but it seemed necessary for the greater good.

"Yeah, right," Aubrey goes. "I'm going to find out what you're really up to, you little freak. Oh, and I'll let Dad know you're borrowing his gloves. I'm sure he'll be quite interested."

I'm like: "I'm sure he'll be even more interested to know how old Chase really is."

Mom and Dad are so blind, they actually believed Aubrey when she told them Chase is seventeen. He's not. I saw his driver's license. He's twenty-two! I can tell Aubrey's a little alarmed that I know this, but she just sticks out her tongue and goes back to her precious Chase, slamming her bedroom door. That's when I decide I better not leave this journal behind anymore, not even hidden behind my framed *Jesus: Don't Leave Earth Without Him* poster. Aubrey's demon might just sniff it out there. So I put it in my knapsack to take along.

When I get to the In-and-Out, Braden's brother Hayden's ancient Camaro is parked outside. It's all brown with one blue door he got from the scrapyard after he accidentally cut the old one in half with a chainsaw. Braden always says that the best thing about having repeated two grades in elementary school is that he's old enough to drive before all of his friends. As if he did it on purpose.

For the first time ever, everyone else is at the In-and-Out before Simon. Braden's wearing rubber boots, but Amelia's got her sister's old Uggs on. I'm like: "Are those water proof?"

"Water proof?" she goes. "I thought the point was to be snakeproof."

I'm like: "It's a bog. Wet."

Braden goes: "Hey, did you hear about those peat bog bodies? They were completely flat because there's some kind of bog-goo that dissolves bones."

Simon gets there finally and he's weirdly flustered; he's usually so Zen. We gather up our tools, the BBQ tongs, flashlights and the Fisher-Price drum and pile into the car. Simon and Braden went on a scouting mission to the bog on Thursday, so they already know the way. They even took the official bog boardwalk tour with a bunch of little kids to find out which part of the bog is the best place to look for snakes.

I start singing the Christian songs to get us in the right frame of mind, but it's not the same without Simon's dulcimer to keep us in tune, so we peter out by the time we reach the bog. We pass by the main entrance, which is all locked up and deserted, and drive around to a gravel road along the far side to park out of sight of the main road. The edge of the bog is surrounded by a chain-link fence here, but it's only about four feet high. We get out with our tools and Braden's already straddling the fence when Simon goes: "Wait."

I go: "We can't waste time, Si. We gotta find one while there's still some light."

But he's like: "I can't do it." He really looks kind of sick and nervous. "I'm scared of snakes."

Amelia's like: "Of course you are. We all are. They're poisonous."

Simon's like: "No, I mean, like even tiny little not poisonous ones. It's not the poison it's the snakes. I don't even like worms."

Braden goes: "You're scared of worms?" and he starts to laugh.

I'm like: "Not helping, Braden," because I've quickly assessed the situation — I'm quite good at that, quickly assessing situations — and it's obvious Simon's not going to change his mind. We're going to have to go in without him, which means we have to rely on Braden to show the way, which means time is even more of the essence because

Braden is more likely to get us lost. I go: "You stay here and keep watch." Simon looks relieved.

Amelia and I follow Braden over the fence. At first the ground is dry, but as we head into the bush it gets mushier until wet mud is sucking at our feet with each step.

Amelia groans: "Oh my God—I mean, gosh, sorry. I've so got bog-goo in my Uggs."

When we reach the boardwalk, Braden's whipping his head back and forth and I can tell he doesn't have a clue which way to go, so I make another quick assessment. I know from Wikipedia that the rattlesnakes are more likely to be where it's dry and rocky, so I suggest we head away from the marshier stuff, toward some birch trees.

Braden goes: "Yeah, this is the right way. Follow me." He keeps doing this. Whenever I make a decision he goes: "Follow me," like it's his plan. Amelia and I roll our eyes at each other.

Where we veer off the boardwalk again the ground is solid, but the sun is going down faster than I expected and it's getting quite dim. I go: "We've got to walk really quietly now, so if we see one, we won't startle it."

Braden goes: "One what?"

Amelia's like: "Snake, you moron! That's why we're here?"

We're creeping forward and it's getting darker and darker, and I have to admit, Jesus, I was starting to have doubts. I started to think, what are we doing here? There was no way we were actually going to find and capture a rattlesnake. But then I remembered what you said, something about faith moving mountains. Finding a snake was kind of like moving a mountain.

So I go: "Guys, I think we need to pray."

We stop and take each other's hands in a circle. Braden goes: "Dear Lord Jesus, so we're here in the bog. We want to pray for the dead people with no bones—"

Amelia elbows him.

"—and most of all for the snakes."

I decide to break in. "Please Jesus, give us faith and guide us. Show us the way. Amen."

Amelia and Braden go: "Amen," and Braden adds: "And thanks a lot, Jesus."

I swear—well, I don't need to swear, because you already know what happened—as soon as I opened my eyes I saw it. I would have shouted Hallelujah, except that might have scared it away. It was right there, between two rocks. No doubt about it. A genuine Massasauga rattlesnake. I know! It was totally crazy! Totally a miracle! I point it out to the others who look absolutely dumbstruck.

Amelia's like: "What do we do?"

I go: "Gloves." I put my dad's gloves on; Amelia's are brown leather; Braden, the dolt, has orange woollen mittens. Amelia has the drum around her neck, so I tell her to take off the lid and put the lid and drum on the ground. Braden has the BBQ tongs. I want to tell him to go ahead and try to grab the snake, but I'm worried about those mittens, not only that they won't block the snake's fangs, but that he won't be able to manoeuvre the tongs without fingers, so I gesture for him to give me the tongs instead.

I was scared, Jesus, I admit it!

So my hands are shaking, and when the tongs first make contact with the snake's body, I nearly drop them. But then the Holy Ghost comes over me. I slide the spatula under the snake and close the tongs as gently as possible around its body. As I lift it up, it begins to squirm and Amelia stifles a little shriek. Slowly, slowly, I shift it over to the waiting drum. It's quite small, only about a foot long, and fits inside the drum perfectly. I try to lift the drum lid with the tongs, but it flips over and I realize I have to move fast to prevent the snake from escaping. Amelia and Braden both gasp as I step forward, pick up the lid with my gloved hand and press it down over the drum before another thought can stop me.

Done. It was done. We had our snake.

I pick up the drum and hand it to Braden who's like: "Cool!" I'm glad, because I'm shaking so much I'm afraid I'll drop it. We have to turn our flashlights on to find our way back to the boardwalk where we argue about which way we came from. I know I'm right, because I took note of a rock we passed that looked like a toad. I shine the light at the ground to see if we can retrace our footprints, but they've already receded into the mud. It's pretty much completely dark by this point. Then I hear this strange thunking sound, so I stop the others. "Wait, what is that?"

We listen, but there's nothing. Until we start walking again and it starts again — it's that moron Braden tapping his finger on the drum with the snake inside. I go: "Braden, what are you doing? You're going to scare the snake?"

Amelia's like: "You're worried about the snake being scared?"

I go: "Just don't agitate it." I'm realizing at this point that we're not on the exact same route on which we came, but I don't want to alarm the others. Suddenly we reach the fence, and there's no sign of Simon or the car. I can't tell whether we've veered to right or left.

Amelia goes: "We could shout his name, see if he hears us."

I'm like: "I don't think it's a good idea to use names. We should have come up with a signal system."

Braden goes: "I could do a monkey screech."

Amelia's like: "There are no monkeys in the bog."

Braden goes: "That's the point. Simon'll know it's me."

Neither of us can come up with any argument against, so Braden goes ahead and does this crazy loud monkey screech that makes Amelia laugh her snorty laugh, which usually cracks me up, but this time I shush her because we have to listen for a reply. It takes a few seconds, but then we hear this weird bellowing sound off to the left. We follow the fence until we see him.

Amelia goes: "What the hell, I mean heck kind of noise was that supposed to be?"

Simon's like: "A cow. Obviously. So ... what happened?"

Braden holds out the drum and goes: "Success!" and Simon runs across the road and pukes all over the grass on the other side. When he finally stops puking, I remind them that we should get a move on in case someone heard the monkey screech and shows up to investigate.

Simon's like: "At least put that thing in the trunk."

Braden goes: "Can't. It doesn't open."

Simon finally agrees to get in the front as long as Amelia and I keep the snake with us in the back seat. We set it between us. Everyone is weirdly silent as we drive back, including the snake, so much so that I wonder if we might have accidentally killed it. But then, as if in response to my thoughts, a soft thrumming sound comes from the drum. I feel it, more than hear it, vibrating ever so softly where the plastic rests against my hip. Amelia must feel it too on the other side, because she goes: "Oh. My. God! Is that——"

I go: "Gosh, you mean. It's nothing."

Simon's all panicked like: "What? What's wrong?"

I'm like: "Nothing. It's nothing," though Amelia and I both know the snake has begun to rattle.

Simon's like: "It's not going to escape, is it?"

Amelia and I both go: "No!" then: "Jinx." We punch each other, but only lightly so we don't jostle the snake.

We all get out at the In-and-Out except Simon, who stays put in the car. He's like: "I can't do it, I just can't do it." He looks like he's going to cry.

So I go: "Look, it's okay, Si, we'll take care of it. Why don't you do some praying?"

He looks relieved. "Yeah, yeah, I'll pray," he goes. He puts his clasped hands together on the dashboard and closes his eyes. The rest of us take the snake inside.

Amelia's like: "How are we going to get it into the terrarium?"

I assess the situation, then put my dad's gloves back on. I put the entire drum inside the terrarium, then reach down and loosen the lid without actually taking it off. I pull the terrarium lid halfway shut. Amelia's watching every move very intently; Braden's rummaging in the cupboard below the counter. I take the BBQ tongs in one hand, and put the other on the terrarium lid, ready to pull it the rest of the way shut very quickly. I grasp the drum lid with the tongs, and just as I'm pulling it aside, Braden—that moron—clangs the cymbals, startling me so much that I drop the tongs into the terrarium. It's Amelia who thinks quickly enough to jump forward and close the terrarium lid.

We both go: "Braden, you're such an idiot!" and punch him. Then we gather around the terrarium to look. The drum is open about a third of the way, wide enough for the snake to emerge, but there's no sign of it stirring.

Braden goes: "Are you sure it's still in there? Maybe it's dead."

I'm like: "It's not dead. It's just scared. Wouldn't you be?"

Braden's like: "No. Not if I was poisonous."

Amelia goes: "My dad's going to kill me if he finds out his tongs are missing. He loves those tongs."

I go: "You'll get them back tomorrow."

We already decided we have to do the ceremony tomorrow, because none of us wants to have to feed the snake any live frogs, which is what they eat.

I go: "Why don't we pray before we go. Braden?"

Braden's like: "Dear Jesus, thank you so much for giving us this snake, and for the food and transportation. Please take care of us all and help us to get Amelia's dad's tongs back. And please help Simon to stop puking. Thanks again. Amen."

"Amen."

I tell the others I want to walk home to work off some of the excitement, and even head across the parking lot and wave while they pass me by in the car.

But I admit, Jesus, it was a little lie. I'm sorry. It's just that I couldn't risk having this journal in the house with Aubrey so suspicious. Unlike her, I sleep like a log, and she knows it. I could have it under my pillow, my head asleep on top, and she'd be able to pull it out without waking me. So once the Camaro disappears, I return to the In-and-Out. I'm nervous, but also a little excited, about being there alone with the snake. When I shine my flashlight at the terrarium, it's still hidden in the drum. I lift the side of the terrarium and feel underneath with a finger: the perfect place to hide my journal!

Thank you, Jesus, for this amazing night. I've got to go now before my parents get home from Hamilton.

Warning to Aubrey: If you are reading this, you are probably about to die from a snakebite. Use the time you have left to confess your sins. No sin is too big for Jesus to forgive — not even stealing the vice principal's car and leaving it in front of the school with a blow-up doll at the wheel. (Hah! You didn't think I knew that was you and Chase. I saw the photos on your phone.) Also, I'm praying for you.

Hi Jesus, Hi Snake. So I'm writing to you both because I can tell the Holy Ghost is present *right in the snake.* I can tell, because I'm not afraid at all. I can put my face right up to the glass and look in its eyes — the only snake in Ontario with vertical pupils, as Simon oh-so-helpfully informed us — and I see you, Jesus. I see you, and I feel love for the snake, just as if it were Grimm the tortoise.

Grimm was the only pet I ever had. My dad is allergic to anything with fur, but my parents still thought Aubrey and I should have the opportunity to learn about taking care of a pet, so they got us Grimm. He is the only person I know who has died. (Well, animal I guess, but he was like a person to me.) It was very sad. Especially when we realized he'd already been dead for several months when we thought he was just hibernating. He was in a shoebox in Aubrey's closet. But she's such a slob, she didn't even notice that something was wrong until the smell was overpowering.

The snake came out of the drum while everyone was gone, and now it's exploring the terrarium in plain sight. Simon's going to freak, if he even comes today. I wanted to get here before the others so I would have a chance to write, and besides, I didn't sleep all night, I was so excited about today. I put on my yellow dress and matching yellow sneakers and little white ankle socks for the occasion. Yellow seems the right colour to wear when I'm filled with the presence of the Holy Ghost, and to hear and channel your voice.

I will never forget the time you first spoke to me, Jesus. Or maybe it was just the first time I listened. It's kind of funny how it all started with that sign that said THE SECRET OF LIFE, given that I discovered the real secret of life that very same day. Every booth at the Grade Nine career fair in the school gym had a whiteboard to tell us what career it represented. Some of the presenters got more creative than others. All of us Grade Niners had to choose three possible career paths, visit the booths, and then write an essay about how they related to our interests and what sort of education and skills we'd have to develop to ... Snore ... I can't even finish that sentence, it's so boring.

Anyway, there's this one whiteboard that says THE SECRET OF LIFE! So I go to that booth, and it turns out the guy is a molecular biologist at Brock University. The guy is so excited to have someone visit his booth; three-quarters of the class, including Aubrey, is gathered around a big plasma screen at the computer animation and special effects booth. The whiteboard there says ZOMBIE APOCALYPSE! The molecular biologist goes into this long spiel about RNA and DNA and I don't even remember what else. Then I'm like: "But what about the secret of life?"

And he goes: "It's all right here! This is the code for life! Mystery no more!"

This made me really depressed. How can the secret of life be a bunch of dead chemicals? But I took an information package anyway, because I needed something to do my assignment with, and the other booths didn't look promising. The second largest crowd was at the Poutini's Poutinerie franchise booth where they were giving out free samples. The smell of the gravy made me feel sick.

Then I see Amelia and some other girls at the PETS booth where there's a woman with a couple of fluff-ball dogs. I have thought a few times about being a vet, so I head over there, but the woman is just a pet groomer from a place called *Dog People*. The girls are taking turns tying ribbons around the dogs' ears. So next I visit the COMMUNICATION booth. I thought that might be about being a war correspondent or writing books, but it turns out communications is just about marketing.

I gave up and went to the student lounge. Simon was already there, taking notes from his information packets, and Amelia comes in right behind me.

I'm like: "Hey Simon. What did you get?"

He goes: "Computer animation, firefighting and audiology—there aren't any musicians out there, so audiology seemed the closest thing."

Amelia goes: "I got pet grooming, software design and poutinerie—that's just cause I didn't have breakfast."

Then Braden comes in and Amelia goes: "Hey Braden, what did you get?"

He goes: "Poutinerie, security guard and pastoral care."

We're all like: *"Pastoral care?"*

"Yeah," he goes. "Nice lady. She gave me a Bible."

He meant the woman with the minister's collar, sitting alone; her whiteboard said SERVICE.

I go: "My grandmother used to ask her Bible questions."

They're all like: "What do you mean?"

So I borrow Braden's Bible to show them how she would ask a question, then close her eyes and let the Bible fall open wherever and touch her finger onto the page. She'd open her eyes and read the exact bit her finger was pointing to. "What do you want to know?"

Simon's like: "Do I have a future as a professional dulcimer player?"

I close my eyes, point to a passage, then read: "Praise him with trumpet sound; praise him with lute and harp."

They're like laughing and: "No way!"

But my scalp was tingling and I showed them it was true. We skipped out of last period to keep asking questions, but not before Simon, Amelia and I snuck back into the gym to see if the pastor had any more Bibles. I didn't sleep that night either.

Anyway, the others are going to be here soon, so I better end and give my journal back to the snake to protect.

Warning to Aubrey: If you're still alive, remember it's never too late to cast Satan out of your heart. Sin is not incurable — unlike a certain STD you got from loverboy. Hah hah hah! Also, I'm praying for you.

⚜

Hi Jesus. So yesterday, Amelia and Braden and even Simon get to the In-and-Out on time, though Simon refuses to come inside, especially once I tell them that the snake is out and moving around. Amelia and Braden are both a bit freaked, but excited too. We roll up the window over the counter so that Simon can participate in everything without having to be inside with the snake. He sits on a milk carton with his dulcimer so we can still sing along to his playing. We pass the wine and bread over the counter when we do our communion, and reach over to grab his hands for prayer.

I take charge and move things along quickly before the energy can dissipate or Braden gets distracted and causes a disaster. We start singing again, softly at first, as we grab hands in a circle around the terrarium, then one by one we lift our hands up to praise you, Jesus.

Then Braden's like: "So who's going to go first?"

I knew all along it would be me, Jesus, and Braden and Amelia look at me because they know it too. Simon keeps playing his dulcimer softly from outside and it's kind of mesmerizing. So I go: "Praise Jesus," in a whisper, and I reach into the terrarium and pick up the snake.

The other two step back from me automatically, eyes all wide, and Braden's like: "Whoa!" Then he takes out his phone and starts snapping pictures. Amelia smacks him, and he's like: "What? She's holding a rattlesnake, man! I've got to take pictures!"

But it doesn't bother me at all, because I can feel the power, the power of the Holy Ghost surging through me. I raise the snake up over my head. I never imagined how good it would feel; I never want it to end.

Then all of a sudden Simon's dulcimer stops, a car door slams, and I hear a loud, dreadful, familiar laugh. Aubrey.

She's calling out: "So this is where you Jesus freaks hang out!"

Simon goes: "You can't go in there."

But Chase is like: "Are you going to stop me?"

There's a thunk and the door flies open, Aubrey screams, and the snake starts to rattle and writhe.

Chase is like: "What the fuck?" He picks up a two-by-four that used to be nailed across the door, and waves it menacingly, like he's going to kill the snake, or maybe me.

I don't have time to think; I just let the Holy Ghost move me. With the snake still in one hand I climb onto and over the counter. Simon sees me and the snake coming and starts to puke, but I don't have time to stop and help him. I run as fast as I can toward the open field that borders the crumbling parking lot. I can hear Chase's footsteps pounding after me, and Aubrey screaming and screaming my name. It must have been making her demon extra mad to see me filled with the Holy Ghost.

I reach the edge and put the snake down in the grass, but it doesn't move. I'm like: "Go, go. Please Jesus go." But it doesn't go; it just stares and stares and I'm like, hypnotized by its power. Then just as Chase reaches me, grabbing me roughly around the waist from behind, it strikes. Amazing, it's like it flies up and latches on to my left calf just above the little white sock. It hangs there for a moment before it shakes free and disappears in the long grass.

Aubrey's screaming: "She's going to die! My sister's going to die!"

Chase is like: "Shut up. We've got to get her to the hospital."

I try to say no, I try to resist, but Chase is too strong, and the fire in my leg is spreading. He hauls me across the parking lot, pushes me into the back seat of his car and makes Aubrey get in with me so I won't escape, even though she won't stop screaming and screaming.

I must have passed out then, because when I wake up in the hospital it's evening. My parents are there; so's Aubrey, with puffy and swollen eyes. But my first thought is of my journal. "Where's my stuff?" I go.

My mom's like: "Your stuff? Amelia took your knapsack with her. She said your phone and your wallet are inside."

My phone and my wallet, but not the journal. My journal is under the terrarium, now devoid of its guardian snake.

I just want to get out of there, but after asking me a bunch of dumb questions and getting me to wiggle my fingers and toes, the doctor says I need to stay in overnight for observation before she's comfortable letting me go.

So after they leave, I fall asleep again. My body's so sore and heavy, full of who-knows-what antivenin drugs. But I will myself awake in the early hours of the morning, so I can escape before anyone stops me. My yellow dress is all wrinkled from being bunched up in the cupboard beside my bed, but it's a lot better than the hospital gown with the slit down the back. The dress still exposes my lower leg, which is all red and purple and swollen to the size of a small watermelon. Only my right sneaker fits on my foot, because my left foot is too fat. I manage to sneak past the nurses who are busy trying to calm a toddler screeching in the next room.

I get a couple of strange looks on the elevator. This

one rude lady's like: "What's wrong with you?" with her nose all scrunched up.

So I'm like: "I got bitten by a rat. They think I might have the plague." And she gets off on the seventh floor even though she pressed the button for two. I know, Jesus, I really shouldn't lie like that, but sometimes it's like, totally justified.

So even though I'm limping like crazy, nobody tries to stop me on the way out of the hospital. I have no money with me at all, not even enough for a bus ticket. The In-and-Out's only a few blocks away, but at this point, my leg hurts so much, I'm not even sure I can make it that far. Then another miracle! In the hedge at the edge of the hospital grounds, I find a scooter, one of those two-wheeled things that you stand on with one leg and propel yourself along with the other. It must have been stolen and dumped, so I don't feel too bad about taking it. It's not really stealing if it's already stolen, is it? I figure I can stand my bare, injured foot on the scooter and push with the better one, but it turns out the real muscle strain is in the weight-bearing leg, and it's better to push with the injured leg, even though I keep stubbing my bare toes.

Thank you, Jesus. I would never have made it all the way here without the power of the Holy Ghost!

All the instruments and chalices are gone — I hope Amelia or Simon took them, and not vandals — but the empty terrarium is still here and, Praise Jesus, so's my journal still hidden underneath.

I pray that the snake finds its way back to the bog. I've heard that lost dogs sometimes find their way home based on magnetism, or something like that. I wonder if it's the same with snakes.

I'm so tired, Jesus. I'm just going to rest here on a bean-bag for a bit. The doctor told my parents that the snake probably didn't inject enough venom in my leg to actually kill me, but I know that's not true. I know it was a miracle, because while I was unconscious, I had a Near Death Experience. There was a tunnel and a bright light and Grimm was there, alive and well. It's a bit fuzzy. I'm hoping maybe I'll recover some more memories about it later, because I know you must have sent me back here for a reason, Jesus. Even exhausted and in pain as I am now, I can feel the Holy Ghost and I know that I have a special purpose. I will figure it out soon, I'm sure.

I'd better get home now before people notice that I've disappeared. I've got to find a new hiding place for my journal, and I'm thinking of printing out one of Braden's photos of me with the snake and gluing it to the cover. Maybe that will scare Aubrey off. But just in case …

Warning to Aubrey: I'm going to hack into your Facebook page, delete Chase's name, and write that you are in a relationship with Jesus Christ. Hah hah hah! Also, I'm praying that it will be true.

Stan's Search for Meaning

"The cosmological argument for the existence of God claims that everything must have a cause separate from itself. If the only thing that can exist outside the universe is God, then God must be the universe's cause," Pamela said, exiting the bathroom on a wave of steamy, grapefruit-scented air from her shower.

Stan opened his eyes. Pamela had married him on the condition that they never engage each other in small talk. Until he met Pamela, Stan had thought of himself as painfully shy. But when he heard her seminar at the local public library, "How Meaningless Chatter Melts the Mind," he realized that the dread he experienced every morning when he arrived at the peanut-butter plant and took up his station on the assembly line across from Louise was born not out of fear of his bubbly colleague, but of the exchange of empty niceties that would take place before the machines came on loud enough to drown her out. Louise was never content with a simple "Good-morning, Stanley." It was inevitably followed by "How are you this morning, Stanley?" to which the rules of the game required he not only lie and say he was fine—when in fact his soul was shrivelling up tighter by the day—but also inquire after her own well-being. No, Stan was not shy; he was deep.

"But the premise of the argument is a fallacy," Pamela said, wriggling her backside into her skirt and pulling up the not-quite-centred zipper. "If everything must have a cause apart from itself, then what caused God?"

Stan blinked several times to shift his mind into gear; he wasn't naturally a morning person like Pamela was. He listened to the rasp of her nyloned thighs rubbing against each other as she retreated briskly down the hall to the kitchen before he rolled out of bed and padded to the bathroom. Brushing his teeth, he nearly gagged on the dry chunks buried in the slug of toothpaste. Pamela's disdain for small talk spilled over into other spheres of minor social niceties, like closing the cap on the toothpaste tube. But it was a small shortcoming Stan was quite willing to forgive; meeting Pamela had been his salvation.

By age forty, he'd worked his way up to Head Peanut Placer, in charge of putting the peanut in the top of each jar before it was sealed, which was pretty much the pinnacle of peanut butter assembly. There was nowhere to go from there until retirement. He'd wandered into Pamela's seminar by accident; in retrospect, he considered it fate. Now he and Pamela spent every free moment, evenings, weekends and holidays alike, working on their masterpiece *A Compendium of Meaningful Topics*. Given the wash of trivial chatter the world was drowning in, the *Compendium*, the antidote, was sure to be a bestseller. They were going to save the world from small talk.

Stan believed the *Compendium*'s success would also free them from their tedious, mind-numbing jobs. Pamela's job was hardly better than his own; she was the receptionist at a company that specialized in manufacturing plastic grass used to beautify takeout sushi worldwide. She had to answer the phone countless times each day with the soul-destroying greeting: "Festive Fakes! How can we decorate your plate?"

Stan couldn't wait for the day he would leave the factory, and Pamela would leave Festive Fakes behind for the last time. It would be soon, he felt sure of it. With the Christmas holidays rapidly approaching, they'd have extra time to work on the book, maybe even complete the first draft. They were currently tackling the concept of God, which was proving to be more complicated than Stan had anticipated. The section was already longer than any of the other doozies they'd already broached, like Evil, Free Will and Veganism. Pamela was a committed atheist. Stan had assumed he was too, until he really started to think about it. The idea of God, it seemed to Stan, must be the idea of an ultimate purpose and explanation for everything. If that didn't exist, in one form or another, wouldn't it make his and Pamela's quest for meaning pointless?

"What all meaningful topics have in common," Stan had said to Pamela last night after they'd turned off the computers and were getting ready for bed, "is that they place the individual in relation to something greater than him or herself. It's got to stop somewhere. There must ultimately be something beyond which there is nothing greater."

"Why does it have to stop at God?" Pamela had replied,

heedless of the crumbs from her bedtime digestive biscuit that tumbled down her nightgown and would end up, Stan accurately foresaw, in their bed. "You can always take one more step and ask what is the meaning of God?"

Stan lay awake for a long time, scratching.

Pamela was already seated at the kitchen table when Stan entered. As he leaned in to kiss her cheek, she poured milk into her bowl of Puffed Wheat causing a tide of buoyant cereal to overflow.

"Cleanliness is next to godliness," Stan said, and Pamela looked at him sharply. Clichés were considered one of the lowest forms of small talk, hence strictly forbidden. But Stan held up a finger to indicate that his use of the saying was in service of something more significant. "The thinking behind that truism is that God equals order, perfection, while cleanliness is order on a more mundane level. Remember 'Tyger, tyger burning bright ...' How does it go? 'What immortal hand or eye/ could frame thy fearful symmetry.' The elegance, the intelligibility of the universe—maybe it doesn't prove God's existence, so much as it *is* God."

"But is nature really ordered?" Pamela asked. "Or do you just think it should be ordered because you hold that view of God? One misconception feeds the other, and vice versa. Consider the search for the unified field. The Holy Grail of physics that will solve the fundamental contradiction between general relativity and quantum mechanics. They haven't found it yet. Maybe it doesn't exist. Maybe the universe is fundamentally messy."

Stan frowned. He'd failed high school physics. He poured himself a cup of black coffee and opened his and Pamela's matching cooler bags to arrange the lunches he'd prepared the night before inside. Tuna sandwich, low-fat yogurt, three oatmeal cookies and an orange. He watched Pamela lift her bowl to her mouth to slurp up the remaining milk, then wiped the table with a dishcloth while she went to the bathroom to apply her lipstick. "We're going to be late," he called, as he put his cup and her bowl in the sink, then grabbed his parka and galoshes.

"But think of how improbable it all is," Stan said, as they hurried to the corner of Queen and Lansdowne where Pamela would catch the westbound streetcar, while Stan took the bus going north. "All the billions of coincidences that had to occur to produce the universe, to produce a planet that would support life, to produce us!"

"It depends on the sample size," Pamela said. "A one-in-a-billion event isn't all that improbable if there are billions of chances for it to occur."

Stan frowned. His grasp of statistics wasn't much better than physics.

"Look!" Pamela pointed. "Our streetcar and bus arriving at exactly the same time. What are the odds of that?"

When he arrived at his station on the assembly line, Louise was already there, wearing a green and white elf's hat covered with bells. "Good-morning, Stanley! How are you this morning?"

"Fine," he said and gritted his teeth, determined to forestall any further chat.

"Well, I'm just wonderful! Wonderful!" Louise said. "I just love this time of year. The most wonderful time of year. Are you all ready for the holidays?"

He smiled vaguely and pretended to be very concentrated on pulling on his rubber gloves while counting the seconds before the assembly line would shift into gear and drown Louise out. When it did, Stan realized that although he could no longer hear Louise's voice, he could still discern the bells, which she continued to ring by nodding like a bobblehead. All morning long.

For many, Stan thought, it was the existence of suffering in the world that precluded the possibility of an all-powerful, all-caring God. Was it just out of desperation that he began to wonder, as the hours in the peanut butter factory dragged on, whether suffering might have some ultimate purpose, even if human beings were not yet equipped to understand it? Wouldn't that suggest that there must be a God who understands what humans do not?

At noon, Stan took his usual seat in the far corner of the lunchroom, as far from the others as possible. But Louise began making her way around the room with a tin of homemade gingerbread men, so he took out his phone. It might not be possible to avoid the cookies, but he could at least preclude conversation if he was already so engaged. He called Pamela at work.

"Festive Flakes! How can we —"

"What about altruism?" Stan asked. "Only something

other than natural selection could explain humans acting against their own interests for the sake of someone else or an idea of greater good."

"It is just as possible for altruism to be favoured by evolution as selfishness," Pamela said. "People who help their families and communities are most likely to be helped in return, which improves their chance of survival and passing on the altruism gene — if such a thing exists," Pamela said.

Stan frowned. Louise was now standing in front of him. He loathed gingerbread, but figured it would be easier to take one and encourage her to move on while he continued his private conversation, but when he reached for the tin, Louise nearly snapped the lid shut on his hand.

"Oh, no, Stanley, that's the wrong one. This one is you, see? I made it to look like you."

Stan stared at the cookie she was pointing to. She'd used a gummy worm to depict his unibrow and eschewed the standard cookie-cutter to give his body a more accurate pear shape.

"Are you still there?" Pamela said into his ear.

A few months ago they'd spent Thanksgiving weekend hashing out the topic "How do we know that we exist?" So this cookie is proof, Stanley thought, reluctantly accepting the chubby gingerbread man. Louise refused to move on until he bit off his own head.

It was already getting dark when Stanley caught the bus home. He sank his chin into the collar of his warm coat and turned to the window to discourage anyone from attempting to discuss the weather with him, as they did amongst them-selves with such endless enthusiasm. Still, he was not im-mune to the tingle of anticipating the first snowfall of the season. That Christmas feeling, was how he still thought of it, though he and Pamela observed no religious holidays.

Even if there was no ultimate purpose to life, no God or concept to explain and justify it all, wasn't it just better to live as if life had meaning, he wondered. A variation on Pascal's wager: You might as well believe life is meaningful. If it turns out you're wrong and the universe is meaningless, then it won't matter. Right or wrong, you'll have felt a little better along the way.

The promised flakes began to fall as he walked the block from the bus stop home, lifting his mood. It seemed Pamela was in a good mood too; Stan found a trail of her work clothing to the bedroom from which she emerged in an alluring black teddy.

"Isn't it ironic," she said, as she reached down and un-buckled his belt, "that the term Platonic is often used to mean nonsexual, when in fact, Plato's ideas were very sexy indeed?"

"You mean the dialectical method?" Stanley said, des-perately trying to recall the topic from last summer to mind. He loosened his tie and allowed her to pull him into the bedroom.

"I mean Plato's theory that humans used to be four-legged, four-armed creatures," she said, pushing him down on the bed and straddling him. "As punishment for discussing how they might climb up to heaven and replace the gods, Zeus split them in half, into male and female. The inference is that one is only complete when joined with one's ideal complement. Oh, Stan!"

"Not just complete," Stan panted. "God-like."

"Oh my God!" Pamela gasped.

For a time, there was no need for any talk at all.

⚜

They had fish fingers and peas for dinner—neither believed in wasting precious writing time preparing meals. When they finished eating, Stan did the dishes and made coffee while Pamela went ahead into the living room, which they had converted into a home office. He brought in two cups of coffee and sat down. They worked at a single, square table, facing each other to facilitate the conversations that generated their material. Each had a laptop. Stan, the faster typist, recorded raw content; Pamela took notes on structure and categorization, and looked things up online. He opened their current file on God. "Going on nine pages now. Shouldn't that mean something, that there are so many arguments for the existence of God?"

"Not if none of them resolves the fact that the very concept of God is fundamentally absurd," Pamela said. "To be conscious, you have to be aware of something separate from yourself. The idea of God is of a being that encompasses everything, which must include consciousness. You see? Consciousness requires separation, but completion includes consciousness. It's a paradox."

Stan felt a migraine coming on. He stood and went to the window to check on the snow's progress. At least a couple of centimetres had accumulated and it was still coming down fast. The family across the street, a couple and two young boys, were all outside putting up Christmas decorations.

Every year they added a new string of lights or a blow-up toy to the gaudy display. The parents were tinkering with something large and round in the middle of the lawn. The boys were running with their heads tilted back and tongues outstretched trying to catch snowflakes in their mouths. Inevitably, they collided and fell.

"Maybe the fact that God is absurd is proof that he *does* exist," Stan mused. "I mean, everything else that exists is."

A snowball sloughed against the window and disintegrated, too fluffy for good packing.

"Everything else is what?" Pamela asked, typing away at her keyboard.

The sphere in the middle of the lawn lit up as the father plugged it in at the side of the house. It appeared to be a giant snowglobe with a carousel of Christmas characters inside. Stan watched Santa go by, then Frosty, followed by a donkey and the three wise men.

"Absurd," he said.

The family clapped and cheered. Stan closed the curtains and returned to his desk.

Acknowledgements

I am grateful to the Ontario Arts Council and the Canada Council for the Arts for grants in support of this work.

"How to Tell if Your Frog is Dead" previously appeared in *The New Quarterly* and in the 2014 Journey Prize Anthology published by McClelland & Stewart.

"Random Swerves" also appeared in *The New Quarterly*.

"'Til Death" appeared in the anthology *That Dammed Beaver* published by Exile Editions.

"Predestination" appeared in *The Danforth Review*.

Many thanks to the editors of all these publications.

I am grateful to Connie McParland, Michael Mirolla and Anna van Valkenburg at Guernica Editions for all the work they do. Thanks also to David Moratto for his cover design.

I want to thank Doug and Nancy Roorda; Dan, Jackie and Joey Roorda; Lindsay Roorda and Ethan Andrews; and Kim and Frank Kessler for all their support.

Thanks also to Sue Chenette, Carolyn Forde, Maureen Scott Harris, Margaret Hollingsworth, Robin Blackburn McBride, Michele Milan, Ruth Roach Pierson, Patty Rivera, Norma Rowen and Nicola Zavaglia.

About the Author

Julie Roorda is the author of three volumes of poetry, and three previous books of fiction, most recently the novel *A Thousand Consolations*.